Touching Lace

Taking friendship to a whole new level...

Lacey Vaughn is tired of being dumped on by men. It's clear she needs help in the ways of seduction. Over cappuccinos, Lacey shares her worries with pal Nick Stone. Being the good friend that he is, Nick offers to give Lacey a few pointers in the ways of sexual pleasure. From his first touch, Lacey forgets all about lessons. Now all she wants is more of his luscious body and skillful touches.

Nick's craved Lacey for months. He's done watching her waste herself on losers. It's time she saw him as more than the dreaded good friend. He'll do nearly anything to have the little spitfire all for himself.

But in order to get Lacey past her insecurities, Nick will have to put it all on the line—including his heart—and pray he doesn't lose her forever.

Warning, this title contains the following: explicit sex using graphic terms. A naughty make-out session in a public place, and lots of steam.

Tasting Candy

Lust was the lure, Candy was the reward.

Walking around with a raging hard-on isn't Blade Vaughn's idea of a good time. He's hungry for sex and there's only one woman on his menu: Candice Warner. When Blade witnesses the shy beauty go into a panic over a harmless encounter, he's more determined than ever to prove that sex with him is just the therapy she needs.

Candice is used to being afraid of her own shadow, but when she goes all nutso in front of Blade, she's beyond mortified. She wants him to see her as an equal, and as a woman. It's time she got over her past trauma and started living again.

But trust is hard to come by when her only experience with men has left her heart in pieces.

Warning, this title contains the following: Hot, steamy, explicit sex. Oral sex. Sex in public places. Oh, and sex in the shower.

Look for these titles by *Anne Rainey*

Now Available:

Haley's Cabin
Burn
Turbulent Passions

The Vaughn Series
Touching Lace (Book 1)
Tasting Candy (Book 2)

Coming Soon:

The Vaughn Series
Taking Chloe (Book 3)

Seduce Me

Anne Rainey

A SAMHAIN PUBLISHING, LTD. publication.

Samhain Publishing, Ltd.
577 Mulberry Street, Suite 1520
Macon, GA 31201
www.samhainpublishing.com

Seduce Me
Print ISBN: 978-1-60504-173-5
Touching Lace Copyright © 2009 by Anne Rainey
Tasting Candy Copyright © 2009 by Anne Rainey

Editing by Linda Ingmanson
Cover by Scott Carpenter

Touching Lace, ISBN 1-59998-903-4
First Samhain Publishing, Ltd. electronic publication: March 2008
Tasting Candy, ISBN 978-1-60504-053-0
First Samhain Publishing, Ltd. electronic publication: June 2008
First Samhain Publishing, Ltd. print publication: April 2009

Contents

Touching Lace

~11~

Tasting Candy

~109~

Touching Lace

Dedication

To my wonderful editor, Linda. I've laughed, I've even pulled my hair, but I'm always grateful to have you in my corner. You've taught me so much and I don't think I'll ever be able to repay you.

To the folks over at The Romance Bistro *After Dark*. Spending my off hours with you has been such a blast! Thanks for letting me share my spicy excerpts. Most of all, thanks for hanging with me.

Chapter One

Things could be worse. Wasn't her mother always telling her that? "*Look on the bright side, Lacey.*" Or her favorite, "*There are lots of people who have things much worse, so be grateful, Lacey.*"

Yeah, she *should* be grateful, actually—grateful she hadn't married the two-timing bastard before finding out about his cheating ways. Catching him beforehand was a definite plus. And to think, she'd thought Christy was her friend.

Lacey sniffled, unwilling to let the tears that burned her eyes fall, and ate yet another chocolate chip cookie—double the chips—and thanked the gods above for creating such a decadent treat to begin with. Tomorrow she would have to exercise double-time just to make up for the damage she was doing to her body today. But for now, comfort food. There wasn't anything quite like it.

As much as she hated to admit it, finding Evan in the shower with Christy happily washing his nether parts, no less, wasn't quite as devastating as it should have been. There was anger—yes, she could have easily taken the two of them apart with her bare hands. But hurt? *Nada.* It seemed like after dating a guy for over six months, a girl really ought to feel at least a twinge of the old heartstrings when she caught him being fondled by another woman. But as hard as she tried, she just couldn't seem to muster any sadness. At least not for Evan. As for Christy, yeah, that hurt.

She'd met Christy one morning while jogging at the park. Christy had overdone it and Lacey had stopped to see if she needed any help. They became fast friends, finding out they had a lot in common. Apparently they even had the same taste in men. Sometimes dating seemed like more trouble than it was worth. It became harder and harder for a girl to find a decent guy.

It wasn't as if her standards were impossibly high. Sheesh! A guy with a decent job. A few morals. Single. And, last but not least, hair. Still, in the past year she'd been dumped twice and cheated on once. That had to be some kind of record.

Maybe it was her. Maybe she was the problem. Her brother Merrick was always telling her she should loosen up some, be a little less assertive. A guy liked to feel dominant, not dominated. She did have a tendency to be a bit controlling, too, now that she thought about it. Lacey ate another cookie as the truth hit her. The one common denominator in every failed relationship was, of course, her.

Then did that mean Evan had hooked up with Christy because Christy was content to let him take the lead? Was that what had drawn him to her? Possibly. Of course, it could just as easily have been her surgically enhanced C-cups.

Swallowing a gulp of milk, Lacey stood and brushed herself off. When she looked down at her own meager chest, she gave a derisive snort.

"The idiot probably thinks Christy's are real. Puhlease."

She grabbed the bag of cookies and started for the kitchen. What she really needed was some vanilla ice cream to go with her chocolate chips. But before she could grab the icy treat, the doorbell rang. So much for completing her sugargasm.

She frowned at the front door. "It better not be Evan." The doorbell rang again and she stomped—which wasn't easy considering she was wearing a pair of fluffy happy face slippers—over to it. Lacey flung the door wide and yelled, "Get lost, dickhead!"

"Pardon me?"

Heat burned her cheeks. "Oops. Uh, hi, Nick."

Nick smiled as if he were pleased as punch. "Do you always answer your door like that?"

She shrugged. "Only when I catch my boyfriend cheating on me with my friend."

"Yeah that sucks. It's also why I'm here." He pushed his way into her apartment. "Get dressed, baby, I'm taking you out."

Bless his thoughtful and sympathetic heart. Nick was one of the sweetest, most honorable, upstanding men she knew. In fact, he ranked right up there with her brothers. Nick was undoubtedly one of the good guys, as well as her best friend. But, right now he was seriously in the way of a very satisfying pity-fest and she just couldn't have that.

"I'm busy, Nick. Get lost, will ya?" She retraced her steps to the kitchen in search of the treasured ice cream. Hopefully Nick would take the hint. She'd almost reached her goal when a hand yanked the back of her sweatpants. "Hey, hands off. I'm not in the mood."

"Too bad. I'm not going to let you eat yourself into oblivion this time."

Lacey pouted. "I'm not eating myself into oblivion."

"Ha! Last time you were dumped, you stayed cooped up the entire weekend eating everything and anything you could get your hands on. Then you exercised yourself to near exhaustion for the next two weeks. Not this time. I just can't take it."

Lacey swatted at his hand and he released her. She swung around and glared at him. "Hey, get this straight. I wasn't dumped. This time I did the dumping." She frowned, "And just how did you know anyway? It was only a few hours ago that I found him with...her." The picture of Christy all giggly and wet and having her way with Evan came crashing back like a bad movie.

Nick cupped Lacey's chin in his hand and stared down at her. She was so beautiful it hurt. So delicate and yet so strong at the same time. Nick wanted to kill the son-of-a-bitch for hurting his sweet Lacey. What kind of man could have her in his bed and still want other women? An idiot.

He rubbed his thumb over her bottom lip and whispered, "Your mom was worried."

"Oh sure, use her why don't you?" she grumbled. "Just what I needed to top the night off right, a healthy dose of guilt."

Nick knew it hadn't been her intention to worry her mom, but he also knew Lacey well enough to realize her first reaction whenever she was hurting was to call her mother. It didn't seem to matter that she was twenty-six; evidently, mom's voice was still a comfort.

"I'm not a glutton for punishment here, baby, so if telling you your mom sent me keeps me out of the doghouse then yeah, your mom sent me." Nick dropped his hand. He was starting to enjoy touching her a little too much. Even with her messy hair and stained sweat outfit, he still wanted to take her to bed. "As good as that outfit looks on you, you might want to change into something slightly less...lived-in."

Nick was intent on getting Lacey over her melancholy, and when he sank his teeth into something, he could be downright tenacious. He smiled at Lacey's sigh of surrender.

"Okay, you win. Where are you taking me?" She turned around and walked to her bedroom.

Nick gave into the smile once she was out of sight. He loved it when she conceded to his demands. It happened so rarely. "I thought we'd go see that movie the dickhead wouldn't take you to."

That had her moving faster. She enjoyed going to the movies. It never got old for her and she was especially fond of thrillers. Damn, he hated to admit it, but he liked that she was available again. It had gnawed at his heart knowing she was with Evan. Thinking of the dickhead making love to Lacey night after night had nearly killed him.

The look of dejection on her face when she'd opened the door had him frowning. Had she cared about Evan so much? Nick hadn't thought she'd been all that into the relationship. If there was one thing he'd learned about Lacey over the years he'd worked for her brother, it was that Lacey fell into relationships more because of the comfort it gave her. She didn't like being alone.

That one little detail had gotten him over to her apartment in record time. With her latest love breakup, he didn't want Lacey to find someone else before he had the opportunity to show her how good they would be together. He had one shot to prove they could be friends *and* lovers.

Nick had figured out pretty damn fast that he had it bad for Lacey. At first, he'd liked her quirkiness and her unconventional ways. They'd somehow fallen into an easy friendship right from the start. In fact, he felt closer to her than he did her brother, Merrick.

Lacey was the only woman he'd ever known who was so comfortable in her own skin. She wasn't insecure or dependant

17

and he admired the hell out of her for those qualities. But beyond that was her sense of fairness and her almost painful honesty. The idea of cheating on your significant other would never even occur to her. He clenched his fist and wished he could thump something or someone in the head. Lacey should have been spared walking in and finding Evan with her supposed friend.

He'd never cared much for Christy. She was too flighty for his taste, and too helpless. He grunted. Yeah right, she was about as helpless as a barracuda. He had run into her a couple of times at Lacey's apartment and she had come on to him both times. Nick hadn't even been tempted. Christy was too in-your-face for his liking. Now Lacey, ah yeah, she was definitely to his taste. Her allure was subtler, classier. Delicate and teasing on the surface, but unrestrained and wild underneath.

He knew deep in his bones Lacey would be a fiery little thing in bed. She wouldn't hold back anything. And Evan had experienced her passion for the past six months. Six months of making love to Lacey. He could kill the bastard for that alone. But what perplexed him to no end was that having Lacey apparently hadn't done it for him. He'd needed Christy, too. No accounting for taste. The more for me, Nick thought happily.

"Okay, I'm ready. But I warn you I'm not the best company tonight."

Nick turned at the hesitant sound in Lacey's voice. She was wearing a little pink t-shirt and jeans. Tight jeans. Christ, she had nice legs. But the slump in her shoulders was enough to stop his raging hormones in their tracks.

Nick crossed the room, pulled her into the cradle of his arms and rubbed the top of her head with his lips. "You don't need to be on good behavior around me, Lace. Remember that."

"Thanks, Nick. You're always such a good friend to me,"

she said softly, clearly meaning every word. "You can't know how much that means."

He felt those words like a kick in the gut. Damn it, he didn't want to be her buddy. He wanted to be her lover. The very best lover she'd ever had. But she never saw him that way, not even from the beginning of their relationship. Well, after tonight she would. He'd see to it. Things were going to change.

He pulled back and cupped her chin in his hand, forcing her to look at him. "After the movie, you and I are going to have a little chat. Whether you want to or not, Lacey Jean."

Uh-oh, things were getting serious, he was calling her Lacey Jean. A rarity for Nick. Although she couldn't even begin to guess at what could be so important. He was always joking and laughing with her. She didn't see this side of him often. Her stomach did a little flip at the intensity in his eyes and the deep tone of his voice. He really was very handsome. So tall and strong. She could easily see why women found him so appealing, so sexy.

Whoa there, girl. This is Nick, remember? Your very best friend in the world, whom you dearly love. She didn't dare wreck that by getting all hot. Rebound stuff, nothing more. She was just feeling raw tonight.

But when she went to retrieve her purse, she could swear she felt his gaze on her backside. Dang, she must have been feeling more vulnerable than she thought if she was imagining Nick eyeing her in that way. He treated her like a little sister, not an attractive female. Which was just fine by her; she didn't need to start seeing things that weren't there.

Lacey grabbed her keys, slung her purse on her shoulder, and they left the apartment. They argued over who was going to drive, as usual. Nick won, which wasn't so usual. Lacey knew she wasn't herself when she put up only a token protest.

Twenty minutes later, Lacey sat next to Nick in the dark theater, their gazes glued to the beautiful actress on the screen. A particularly nasty part in the movie had her jumping in her seat and Nick reached over and took her hand. At first, his touch felt familiar and comforting, but when he brought her hand to the top of his thigh and held it there, something altogether different raced through her body.

His muscular leg was firm beneath her fingertips, and her hand automatically began to stroke and knead. He must have liked what she was doing because she swore he groaned. It was the kind of guttural sound that made her think of naked bodies and tangled sheets. Darn it, she was doing it again. Going where she shouldn't be going—sexual territory—and it was strictly off-limits for her and Nick.

Lacey attempted to yank her hand away, but he wouldn't let go. Finally, she took a deep breath, turned and looked into his eyes. She was stunned at what she saw there.

Desire. Dark, deep, sexual heat. For her?

How could that be? Nick had never acted even remotely attracted to her. He'd teased and flirted, but that was a guy being a guy. Was she only seeing what she wanted to see? No, that wasn't it. She knew when a man was turned on and Nick was definitely turned on. She simply didn't know what to make of this new turn in their relationship.

Then, to her continued surprise, Lacey watched as Nick's lips slowly tilted upward, as if daring her to carry on with her exploration. When she stayed still and unmoving, he released her. Okay, he wasn't going to force the issue. Part of her was glad.

Part of her wasn't.

She leaned back in her seat and desperately tried to

become engulfed once again in the cheesy horror, but she couldn't get her mind off that gaze. The fiery intensity and his challenging grin afterwards. He'd be something in bed, no doubt. Hmm, she wondered what he'd meant earlier when he'd said they were going to have a little chat.

Lacey wasn't sure she could handle a man like Nick. Panic crept in at the thought of being on the receiving end of someone with such a passionate nature. If there was one thing she knew about herself, it was that she was a total sissy when it came to alpha males. And Nick was every bit the alpha.

It hadn't bothered her before, because with her, he was always laid back and easy going, but she'd seen him when he was attracted to a woman. He could be downright ruthless. Nick would effortlessly toss convention and political correctness to the wind and do whatever was necessary until he got what he wanted.

The question Lacey couldn't get out of her mind was, what did Nick want now?

Chapter Two

They sat in Turro's, a little coffee shop close to Lacey's apartment, eating apple cobbler and drinking cappuccinos. She was being so meek and quiet. Nick couldn't help but smile. She was never meek and rarely quiet. His little maneuver in the theater had gotten to her. Good, let her ponder it a bit, wonder at his motives. Lord knew he had been pondering and wondering over his attraction to her for what seemed like an eternity. She owed him.

Nick decided to start with the topic of her recent break up. "So, as you already know I got the low down from your mom about Evan, but I'm all ears if you want to talk about it."

Lacey looked up sharply, her pretty blue eyes revealing just the slightest hint of pain. Had he misread her relationship with the dickhead? Could it be she had real feelings for him? He'd thought she was more upset over the loss of her friendship with Christy than losing Evan. Now he wasn't sure.

Nick reached across the scarred wood table and just barely touched her fingers. "Did you love him, Lace?" He nearly got sick at the thought of her wasting those kinds of feelings on a loser like Evan, but he needed to know what he was up against.

Lacey's easily given kindness shone in her gorgeous eyes. He knew she was seeing her best friend in the whole world sitting across from her. She probably saw the worry he felt staring back. Her sweet smile was the same as always and had the same impact to his libido as ever. As usual, Nick hid his unfriend-like reaction, and he hated it.

"No, I didn't love Evan." She wrinkled her nose. "I guess that's the saddest part. I didn't even feel the slightest bit hurt when I caught them sponging each other up." She laughed, and his body reacted to the throaty sound. "Oh, Nick, you should have seen them. Their ridiculous expressions, so shocked, and all I could think was 'oh well, saves me the trouble of dumping him'." She tried to laugh again, but sobered instead. Her expression beat at him.

His Lace was feeling a cruel stab of insecurity, and he hated it. She looked down at her cobbler; like him, she'd all but forgotten it.

"What's wrong with me that men find it so easy to dump all over me?" Lacey's question surprised him. She dropped her spoon in her bowl where it made a loud clang then crossed her arms over her chest and continued her angry outburst. "Why can't I seem to hold a guy's attention for more than a few pathetic months?"

First, Nick wanted to shout with glee because she hadn't loved the idiot. Second, he wanted badly to shake her and rattle some sense into her. She'd damn well held *his* attention for a lot longer than a few meager months. But he'd only scare her away.

"You're not to examine yourself over this guy, Lace." He dropped his own spoon, pulled her arms apart and entwined their fingers. "There isn't a damn thing wrong with you. It's the men you date. They aren't worth the air you breathe, baby."

Lacey only shook her head in denial. "No, Nick, that's not true. They can't all be losers." She gave him a half-smile. "Though I appreciate your undying loyalty."

"It's not loyalty." She didn't look convinced, so he changed tactics. "You say it's you, right?" She shrugged, neither confirming nor denying. "Then explain to me what it is you think is wrong with you."

Nick began to stroke his thumb over her wrist and he could feel the quickening of her pulse as it jumped wildly. As if uncomfortable, Lacey took back one of her hands, and he very nearly groaned aloud.

"It's a little complicated."

Nick frowned. She was keeping something from him. He could always tell. Lacey was never very good at deceit. She gave herself away every time by looking down toward the ground. "Uncomplicate it for me then."

She tilted her head. "Is that even a word?"

"Don't change the subject. Explain why you think every man you date ends up bored."

A pretty bloom of pink filled Lacey's cheeks at his personal question. Even as close as they were, he was still a guy, thus making such a conversation uncomfortable. This time he wasn't going to let it slide. Nick wouldn't allow her to bury her head. Lacey knew him like no one else, which meant she knew deep, meaningful conversations didn't scare him off the way they did most men. Hell, with Lacey, going deep was a damned pleasure.

"I don't think I'm very good in bed. There, is that plain enough for you?"

Lacey's words were so rushed Nick would have missed half of what she said if he wasn't so attuned to her. Luckily, Lacey couldn't lose an eyelash without him taking notice.

Of all the reasons for her sudden lack of confidence, that had never once crossed his mind. Now he knew for sure she was picking the wrong men. Lacey's feisty attitude and easy sensuality would make her nothing short of explosive in bed.

Hell, a man would have to be blind not to see the passion and fire that simmered just beneath the surface. It would take years for a man to get bored with a woman like her. Nick suspected she didn't have a single problem, but how could he prove it to her?

It was true a sensual and uninhibited woman like Lacey could intimidate someone like Evan. Even cause him to turn to a woman like the overblown and too obvious Christy. The loser probably needed to be in control to stoke his ego. Yep, the guys Lacey chose were clearly wusses. Otherwise, they'd know what to do with the dark-haired beauty who fairly shouted *flaming hot sex!*

Her sexual confidence had been shaken and it pissed him off enough to want to pay a little visit to Evan the Dickhead. And that's when a plan began to form.

She didn't think she could heat up the sheets worth a damn. Well, who better to teach her how completely wrong she was than a man she already cared for and trusted? He mentally squashed the little voice in his head, which vigorously shouted to him just how wrong this plan of his could go. Now to convince the stubborn and hardheaded Lacey Vaughn that her good buddy always knew best.

"Lace, look at me." He waited for her eyes to meet his. "I think I know how to get you over your silly insecurities."

"Believe me, I'm all for any advice you can give me. It's pretty clear I need help."

He pretended to consider her problem then he leaned in closer until he was a mere breath away. He could smell her clean scent; she wasn't all perfumed like most women he dated. It seemed he never got enough of Lacey's fresh femininity.

Very softly, so as not to spook her, he said, "What you need is a healthy dose of sexual confidence."

She looked ready to bolt. Oh, Lacey wasn't shy, not with two rowdy older brothers to learn from, but neither was she comfortable discussing sex so openly.

"You said yourself you aren't very...adept at mattress calisthenics," he said.

She covered her mouth, chuckling at his description. He loved the way her face lit up just for him. At least he liked to think it was just for him. "What would you say to me giving you a few private lessons?"

In a rather strangled voice, Lacey asked, "Are you saying what I think you're saying, Nick?"

He sighed, beyond frustrated, and growled out, "I don't think I quite like the skeptical look on your pretty face. Hell, most women find me rather handsome. Even sexy and charming. Yet you look right through me as if I'm sexless. Damn it, Lace. I want you to see me as a man. A man you can't resist."

He pushed their long forgotten cappuccinos aside, grabbed her arms and pulled her until she was half lying on the little table between them then kissed her. It wasn't a gentle, friendly peck, either, like the kind he usually gave her. This kiss was hard, demanding. A searing meeting of lips meant to drive his point home in the most basic way possible.

He hadn't known she would taste so good. He hadn't been prepared for her. Her mouth was deliciously addicting. This was what he'd been missing in every single one of his other relationships. This was the woman he'd been aching to have.

Take it slow, he reminded himself. He drew back a little, enjoying Lacey's moan, but smothered it quickly with another kiss. They were in a coffee shop, and he definitely didn't want an audience when he gave Lacey a taste of real passion for the first time.

"Is that clear enough for you?" he asked.

She couldn't speak, couldn't think. Her heart pounded out of her chest and her blood raced through her veins. In the theater, she'd thought it her imagination that Nick might be showing her something besides friendship. She'd stroked his thigh, and he'd groaned. Lacey thought she'd been reading too much into the simple touch, but now she was beginning to see Nick might truly want her. His demanding and possessive kiss had made that crystal clear.

Lacey met Nick's stare. He still waited for her answer. "Uh, yeah, I think you made your point."

Was that her husky voice? Lacey touched her lips and felt Nick's warmth lingering there still. Oh my, what would it be like to have him naked? Nick on top of her. Underneath her. Inside her. It was all starting to sound rather exciting. She had a feeling he'd be magnificent. And he did have a point, she did need lessons. But what would happen to their friendship?

He reached over and took her chin in the palm of his hand. "I'd never hurt you, baby. We could take it as slow and easy as you want. I promise you can trust me, Lacey." His whisper turned her knees into a weak imitation of Jell-O.

He sounded so sure, so convincing, but she needed to know where his sudden desire for her was coming from. She sat back, forcing him to drop his hand. "Nick, why do you want to do this? What do you get out of these lessons?"

It sounded strange, arranging to have private sex lessons with her best friend. Weirder still, not as strange as it should. She was still burning from the kiss. The thought of going further, deeper, was wildly intriguing. He was her friend, and friends didn't have sex together. It wasn't to be considered.

So, why was she so excited?

Nick looked startled, as if she'd just asked him to stand on his head in the middle of Main Street. Then, with a look that singed her eyelashes and in a voice ripe with lust, he growled out, "Are you kidding me? Damn, Lace, what I get is *you*. Haven't you figured out yet that I want you?"

As her mind absorbed his shocking words, her body snapped to attention. He'd never given her any indication he was even remotely attracted to her. As she stared at the shape of his mouth and then the hotter than hot look in his anxious eyes, she realized he was well beyond ready to take her home and have his way with her.

"Yeah, baby, I want you. And you'd better start getting used to the idea, because I want you gloriously naked and all mine. In every way I can think of and for as long as possible."

Oh, God. It was all too much. Lacey blinked, dazed and even a little bit afraid, if she was being totally honest. She hadn't expected to feel anticipation uncurling in the pit of her stomach, but oddly enough she liked the idea of getting down and dirty with Nick. She'd wondered a couple of times, when they'd double dated, what it would be like to have all that feral masculinity focused her way. To have his strong hands touching and stroking her body. His eyes staring at her with dark promise.

She'd wondered, but it never occurred to her he might have wondered, too. "Nick, what if things don't turn out so well? I would die if anything hurt our friendship. I care about you too much to let sex ruin that."

Nick's predatory smile sent a shiver of awareness up her spine. "We are two intelligent adults. We can handle this." Her indecision must have shown on her face because he pushed a little harder. "I want to see you naked. I want to touch you, to taste you...all over." He lifted his fingers to her neck and stroked her erratic pulse with his thumb. "Christ, just the thought of having my cock inside you, tight and wet, makes me so hard I hurt," he said gruffly. "Please tell me I'm not the only one feeling this way, baby."

Lacey couldn't think, couldn't move. A few heated words from Nick and she was on fire. Ready and aching for everything he could give her. Eager to meet his every demand. It had never been this way for her before. Then again, Nick wasn't just any man. She swallowed convulsively and whispered, "No, you're not the only one."

Nick's gaze roamed over her, a slow caress. Lacey burned from the inside out. His eyes touched on her breasts. Her breathing grew rapid. Her chest rose and fell. As she sat there, her nipples hardened just for him. A blatant enticement beneath the fabric of her t-shirt.

"Are you wet for me right now, Lacey?" His tone was gentle.

"Nick! We shouldn't be talking like this in public."

His jaw went rigid. "No more restraints, that's lesson number one. Let go of your embarrassment. With me, nothing is taboo."

She gave that a quick thought then took the plunge. "Yes, Nick, I am wet. And..." she said huskily, "and I want desperately to be alone with you right now."

He started to rise from the table, and suddenly her fear of losing him as a friend caused her to reach out and grasp his forearm, just barely stopping him from dragging her out of the diner.

"But I'm not ready for this. Not so soon. I need some time to consider the ramifications of what you're proposing. Please understand."

Nick plopped back down in the seat, as if defeated. Lacey simply couldn't take the look of raw need on his face.

"I'm not saying no. Just...not yet," she pleaded, gently willing him to understand he was moving too fast.

For long seconds Nick only stared at her, not saying a word as the tension between them grew. She feared she'd made a grave mistake, but she couldn't let him overpower her. He had a way of pushing and prodding until he got his way. This time, however, she couldn't let him win.

"Okay. I'll take you home."

"Thank you." Lacey let out a long breath, not entirely sure if she was happy or sad that he'd given in to her wishes. Then he reached over and cupped her chin, forcing her to look up and into his warm brown eyes.

"I'm not giving up. I'm only giving you some time to get used to the idea."

Lacey smiled, a genuine smile of understanding for the man who had been her best friend for the past five years. "I've never known you to give up."

He winked, and his face turned from serious to fun loving, giving her a glimpse of the man she'd gotten to know in a way she didn't know another living soul.

"And just so we're straight, for the time being you and I are exclusive. That means I'm the only man you'll call if you feel all hot and horny in the middle of the night."

A laugh bubbled up and she felt herself slipping back into the comfort zone she'd grown accustomed to. "You are way too arrogant for your own good, Nick Stone."

"Arrogance has nothing to do with it, baby. It's all about confidence." 'His voice came out as an erotic whisper. "And I'm confident I'll win you over. It's just a matter of time. The clock is already ticking."

Nick rose from the table, tossed a few bills down to pay for their drinks and cobbler then held out his hand for Lacey. She looked at it, unsure and even a little bit afraid.

"Come on, I'll take you home...so you can think about what I've said."

Very slowly, Lacey pressed her fingers into his much larger ones, twining them together then smiled up at him. He looked so sweet, so ruggedly handsome, and she became acutely aware of their size difference.

Lacey had never given it a thought before, but now that their relationship was trekking into new territory and she was so close to being in his bed, it was all she could think of. Would he be so big and hard all over? Would he be a gentle lover, or demanding and wild? Or, even better, both.

Lacey only hoped she could maintain her distance until she had more time to think. Good God, she was already imagining having sex with him, and she hadn't even agreed to anything yet. What was wrong with her?

As he walked ahead of her, pulling her out to his SUV, giving her an enticing glimpse of his perfectly sculpted ass, she knew exactly where her mind had gone. She reminded herself to think over his proposition.

Chapter Three

Once they were on their way in Nick's Black SUV, Lacey took her time looking her fill. She knew what she had always seen when they were friends, but now, seeing Nick as a potential lover, showed her things she had never known were there.

The hard angles of his face, now cast in the blue light from the dashboard, made him look sinful. His dark hair was in need of a trim as small tendrils kept dropping down onto his forehead. It looked sexily mussed, and Lacey could easily picture him the morning after a long and pleasurable night of loving. She wiggled around in her seat, attempting to squelch her body's enthusiasm to the carnal image.

Nick's skin was darkly tanned from all the time he spent outdoors. He was heavily into sports of all kinds. He and her brother, Merrick, did a lot together on the weekends. He also worked out at her gym. His ripped six-foot two frame was proof that good eating habits and plenty of exercise did indeed do a body good.

He had perfect, sculpted muscles—not huge, but fit. Her gaze landed on the fly of his jeans and Lacey nearly whimpered.

He was aroused. Splendidly aroused. God, she hadn't known he was so big. Even through his jeans, she could tell he was larger than any man she'd ever known. Right under her nose all this time. It made a lady's heart flutter in awe.

He turned toward her and she was struck by the primitive grin on his face—as if he could read her every thought. Her face heated furiously.

"Look all you want, baby," he whispered dangerously, "but sometime, hopefully soon, it'll be my turn to look."

Dispel the tension, Lacey chanted to herself. They both needed to get things under control or they would be pulling over and having at it on the side of the road. She really wasn't into voyeurism.

"Nick, do you believe in magic?" She hadn't a clue as to where in the world that thought came from. Since the question was out there, though, Lacey had to admit she was a little curious as to what sort of things ran through Nick's mind. What was he into? What turned him on?

He cocked his head, but never took his eyes off the road. "What, like David Copperfield?"

She rolled her eyes. "Not smoke and mirrors, but real, everyday magic." He looked at her and arched a brow as if to say, "Huh?" So, she explained. "For instance, last week when you helped the woman at the grocery get her car started, that was magic." Nick was such a gentleman, and privately she'd always thought of him as a white knight.

He scoffed. "No, that was a piece of shit battery."

She shook her head. "I don't think so."

Nick frowned. "Then what do you think it was?"

"I think it was magic. The fact that you were there to help her. She had four kids, what was she going to do?"

He shrugged, as if not entirely comfortable with the conversation. "I believe in what I can see. You know I have to see it to believe it, Lace."

"Yeah? Then what about love? You can't see it, but you believe in it don't you?" She knew he did, because he'd once told her he wanted to get married and have kids. He didn't like the idea of being a bachelor when he was old and gray. Now that she thought about it, she could easily picture Nick with a couple of little squirts running around. He'd make a wonderful father.

Very softly, he answered, "I believe in love. I'm just not sure what magic has to do with it."

"Nick, I'm surprised at you." She turned in her seat to see him better. "Love is magic in its rawest form." She lowered her voice, speaking in a near whisper. "A touch that sends your pulse racing, or a look that goes straight to your soul. Those aren't things you can explain away with chemistry and science. Its magic."

Okay, so she was into mystical mumbo-jumbo. He could work that to his advantage.

And damn she had a sexy voice.

He took his eyes off the road for a moment and glanced at Lacey. A small part of him believed in what she said. He really wanted to admit the truth. Hell, yes, he believed in love. He'd been in love with her from practically the beginning of their relationship. But Nick knew she wasn't ready to hear that. The fact she hadn't yet agreed to his plan was reason enough to hold back on his real feelings. One thing was obvious. Lacey was wound up and excited by the idea of being intimate with him. Nick knew a sense of primal pleasure when he saw the eager delight in the depths of her baby-blues. All her attention was on him tonight. It was enough to send his heart soaring to the heavens.

If he was forced to go home alone, to sleep in a cold bed,

the least he could do is give her a taste of what he'd do to her once she surrendered.

With his eyes back on the road, he feigned a relaxed tone as he murmured, "I see what you mean now. And because I don't want you to think I'm close-minded, how about I tell you my own version of magic?"

Out of the corner of his eye, Nick could see Lacey smiling over at him. His gut clenched in reaction. "Okay, I'm all ears."

It was all the permission he needed. "Magic is going to be taking your clothes off. One small piece at a time, baby. So I can savor the sight of you." He heard her startled breath and he smiled. Damn, he loved surprising her this way. Taking her off guard and slipping in under her defenses seemed the only way to reach the woman who lay just out of his reach.

"Magic is going to be bringing you to climax." He looked at her, and even in the soft glow of the streetlights, he could see the way her face heated at his words. The talking was turning her on. He'd remember that little detail.

"I have a feeling you're beautiful when you come." She started to say something, but Nick turned his attention back to the road and kept right on talking. "It's going to be magic, pure and raw and hot, when I slip inside you for the first time."

He turned his SUV into her apartment complex and shut off the engine. "We're here."

"Uh-huh."

She'd gone speechless, and he reveled in the knowledge. She was always so keyed up, so full of bubbling energy, to see her go all soft and quiet was a score for him. If he wanted to push, he could lean over and kiss her. Maybe entice her into inviting him up. Nick didn't want her that way. He wanted her to want him for who he was. Not just to scratch an itch.

With that in mind, Nick took her hand off her lap, where

she'd been clutching at her jean-clad leg, and placed a small kiss in the center of her palm. "I remember this one time when you tried to cook some gourmet meal for that asshole Jerry. You cut your finger. Right here," Nick murmured, as he kissed the exact spot on the back of her index finger. "You broke up with him shortly after, claiming if it was Susie Homemaker he wanted, he was barking up the wrong dress. All I could think was how sweet your finger tasted against my lips when I kissed your boo-boo." Nick looked back up at her and gruffly whispered, "Sweet dreams, baby."

Lacey stared at him, slack-jawed for a moment then she began to frown in that mutinous way that had him grinning. She turned and opened her door and Nick chose to issue one other little demand.

"I'm not going to walk you up this time. I don't want to be faced with the temptation of having your bed a few feet away. I'll see you tomorrow. We'll meet at the gym and work out. You can give me your answer then, okay?"

Lacey nearly fell out of the door. "Tomorrow?" she squeaked.

"Yes, tomorrow."

"I need more time."

Nick winked at her. His little Lacey was backpedaling big time. "Do you, baby? Hmm, I wonder. How about we see what a good night's sleep brings."

She nodded, her lips firm and her back straight as a yardstick. As she shut the truck door a little too hard, he chuckled.

He watched her quick, even strides as she made her way inside the building. On the rare occasion that he didn't walk her up, she would flip her lights to signal she was safely inside her apartment. Nick waited. When the lights flicked on and he saw

Lacey standing at the window, he revved the engine and drove off, thoughts of her beautiful body filling his head.

Nick had had about enough of watching from the sidelines while she let other bozos have their way with her delectable body. Lacey Vaughn was fair game now. With any luck, by the time he was through with her, she'd see they could have something special together. Because he wasn't about to let her walk away from him and into another man's arms. Not ever again. His heart just couldn't take it anymore.

He could sense her submitting to him, which meant she wasn't quite as immune to his charms as he'd originally thought. A rush of possession ran through him, a foreign feeling for Nick. Apparently with Lacey, as far his emotions went, all bets were off. He had no idea what to expect. She affected him as no other woman ever had.

"Shit. Another cold shower."

As Lacey watched Nick's red taillights fade off into the distance, she became aware of one very important fact. She'd somehow managed to go from the frying pan and into the fire in a matter of hours.

When she'd broached the topic of magic, it was supposed to provide neutral conversation, but then she had to go and mention love. Nick's seductively whispered words heated her body, and she'd forgotten her train of thought as erotic images filled her head. Not that she minded the heat, but coming from Nick, her best bud, it was all so unexpected.

Titillating, but unexpected.

She yanked at her shoes, not bothering to untie the laces first, and flung them aside. She started to pull off her clothes, tossing things willy-nilly, uncaring where they landed. Lacey was too old to change her slobbish ways. All she really wanted was to go to bed and forget about everything.

Slipping into her favorite flannel, penguin pajamas, Lacey replayed Nick's words in her mind. He would expect an answer tomorrow, he'd said. God, the man was simply too much! Did he think she was going to fall into his arms and beg him to take her? Did he really think one night would be long enough for her to consider all the pros and cons of taking a perfectly good friendship and thrusting it to a new level of danger? Well, of course it wasn't enough time.

As she crawled under her white goose-down comforter and flipped off the bedside lamp, Lacey couldn't help thinking about the way his body moved. So fluid and masculine. He was every inch a hard, aggressive male, the kind she normally avoided as a sexual partner. Except in the privacy of her mind. At night, when no one was around, Lacey often let her thoughts wander into erotic territory. Only this time her mind was intent on having Nick fill the position of sexy lover. She'd be in a bucket load of want if her dreams took her where he wanted them to be. Maybe she should stay awake.

Then again, maybe not.

It was her last image of him, as he sat in his SUV staring at her with hunger and desire, all but willing her to come home with him. Her mind saw him there in the darkness, sitting behind the wheel, so strong and virile and so incredibly gorgeous. Slowly, reality fell away and her dream world rose. There were no taboos in the world of dreams. No right and wrong. Only wants being fulfilled, desires being shared. Lacey wouldn't leave him to drive home alone and aching in this world. In her dream, she would stay and take what she wanted.

As with most dreams, one minute they were in the SUV and

the next she lay on her bed, naked. Nick was on top of her, staring down at her with a kind of craving she'd never seen on a man's face. He spoke, but she couldn't understand the words. All she knew was the way he made her feel. His hands touched her body, drifted and tickled, until they came to rest against her quivering breasts. He leaned down and sucked one hardened peak into the heat of his voracious mouth. Lacey jolted with the contact.

He pressed into her, slipping only the tip of his cock inside her wet pussy. She wanted nothing more than for him to thrust forward, to take her hard and drive her into oblivion. But he seemed intent on taking his time.

Nick licked and bit at her breasts, using his hands to squeeze and fondle, as if testing their weight in his hands. Lacey reached up and touched his shoulders, his sleek muscular back then lower to his perfect glutes. She was beyond ready for him. Lacey wrapped her legs around his thighs and used her hands to pull him deeper. She wanted him. Needed him to fill her. She ached for him to take away the cold emptiness to which she'd grown so accustomed.

She shamelessly begged Nick, her dream lover, and suddenly he lifted up and stared down at her. Long seconds passed and not a single syllable drifted through his talented lips. He leisurely pushed his hips against her pelvis, driving his huge, throbbing cock so deep their bodies melted together. He clutched her hips, pulled her lower half off the bed, and drove in harder still. Lacey's body began to climb. She watched intently as the play of emotions on Nick's face went from calm and controlled to wild and untamed. In that instant, she let her inhibitions fall away as she revealed to him her own impatient cravings.

He started to pump into her. Harder. Faster. Nick slammed his hips against hers. She cried out in surprise as he reached down and pressed his warm palm flat against the giving flesh of her lower belly. She knew he was able to feel his hard dick inside of her there, pushing in and out of her tight body. His hand touching her in such a possessive way brought tears to her eyes. In some elemental way, her heart and soul entwined with his in that moment.

She started to close her eyes, but his harsh demand had her opening them again. She gazed up at him, uncertain, scared, but in need of what only he could give.

Lacey's aching breasts bounced as Nick fucked her, plunging his engorged cock deep. Inevitably, Nick's eyes were drawn downward. She moaned low when he dipped his head and drew his tongue across her over-heated nipples, drawing little circles around her areolas.

It all became too much. Lacey screamed out her climax. Nick was right there, filling her with his hot come and shouting her name over and over.

At that exact moment, Lacey was yanked from her dream world and brought back to the world of the living with the ringing of her phone.

"Damn it," she muttered as she reached over and nearly shouted, "Hello?"

"Wake up on the wrong side of the bed, did we?"

"Nick?" she squeaked. Her face flushed deep with the thought of where her mind had been all night long. She still vibrated and pulsed with heat. She hadn't had a wet dream like that since her teenage years. Not even then were they so vivid and perfect.

"Yeah. Did you sleep well, baby?"

"Like a rock." Well, what could she say? That she'd just let him have her body as if she was a sex slave and he the almighty sheik?

"Really? Because you sound...agitated."

"Yep, really." She lied with alacrity then sat up and got out of bed. Sliding her feet into her fuzzy happy face slippers, she headed toward the kitchen and coffee. "Was there something you wanted at—" she looked at the clock on her microwave, "—seven thirty in the morning?"

"I dreamed about you last night, Lace."

That stopped her in her tracks. Could he be serious? "Uh, what sort of dream?"

She heard him chuckle. "Let me put it this way. You weren't exactly sitting in a rocker knitting, if you know what I mean."

Her body liquefied at his words. Well, crap. Like she didn't know what he was talking about. Her insides had twisted with lust all night long. "You said you'd give me time to think about this."

"You had all night."

"I was sleeping all night."

"I was, too, with you, moaning and quivering and coming all around my cock. I didn't want to wake up from that."

"Oh." He laughed again, making her snap at him in turn. "What time are we working out? I've got a lunch date, so it'll have to be either before or after that."

"With who?"

Nick's laughter had ceased. Now he sounded downright furious. What was that about?

"No one you know," she said mysteriously, intent on finding out more about this new side to her best friend. Nick the predatory male, the sexy lover, was a foreign notion to her.

"Is it a man? Because I thought we agreed to be exclusive."

Oh my, the man had a rather intriguing jealous streak.

41

Interesting. Pulling out the glass pot, Lacey began rinsing it and decided to put Nick out of his misery. Even if he had dragged her away from the best erotic dream of her life.

"I haven't agreed to anything yet. But, no, it's not a man. Just Patty and Mary. So, don't go all caveman."

"Little witch," he snarled, but his voice did calm, she noticed. "How about four o'clock we meet at the gym? We'll work out together and you can give me your answer then."

"Yeah, that works for me, I guess." Then something strange stirred in her belly as Lacey wondered what Nick had planned for the day. "What are you up to today?"

"I'm going to the office for a bit. There's a big client I've been finessing and I want to take one last look at my sales pitch before Monday comes around. After that, I plan to annoy your brother for a while. Why?"

She heard him take a sip of something, probably coffee. Their mutual love for the dark brew was always something they had had in common. Then his words registered. He was meeting with her brother? Today? For some inexplicable reason the idea gave her a start.

"You're going to see Merrick?"

"Uh, I was considering it. Is there a problem?"

Lacey wondered if there was a problem. He and Merrick were good friends and had been for quite awhile. Guys talked, didn't they? Would Nick tell Merrick about the new twist in his relationship with her?

Then, as if reading her thoughts, Nick made a tsking sound. "I don't kiss and tell, baby, you know better."

She did know better and she was a rotten friend for even thinking he would. "Yeah, sorry. But Nick?"

"Yeah?"

"What if things get all muddled? I'm really scared," she admitted in an uncharacteristic show of uneasiness.

"I know you are, but I won't let it get muddled. You only need to trust me, baby. Everything will work out fine. You need a boost of confidence in the bedroom and I'm going to give it to you. Simple as that, right?"

Lacey tucked a filter into the basket. "I don't know. I still need to think about this."

"You always think everything through so thoroughly," Nick reflected with a hint of an indulgent smile in his voice. "I can still remember the time you decided to cut your hair. It was always annoying the hell out of you and getting in the way of your workouts. I wanted so badly to tell you to leave it long. I wanted to have a chance to see it lying against your perfect, naked body. But then you took the plunge and did it anyway. I grieved over that hair. I sat in my house, alone, and drank a six pack as I imagined us having sex with nothing but your hair covering you."

"I never knew. God, I swear I never knew." How could she have been so blind? There was so much more to Nick. Lacey had the uncomfortable notion she'd been seeing her friend in black and white then suddenly someone flicked on a plasma screen and everything took on new dimensions.

"I know. We were friends, sweetheart, and whether you cut your hair, dyed it pink, or wore a Mohawk, it was a decision you had to make for yourself. In the end, it worked out fine, because I can still imagine fucking you, only now your hair isn't in my way."

Lacey clutched at the phone and groaned aloud. "Nick, you are seriously driving me crazy with all these little bombs you keep dropping on me!"

"Four o'clock?" he asked, hope and tenderness in his deep,

sexy voice.

She sighed and gave in. "Yeah, I'll be there."

They hung up, and Lacey was able to move again. She went to the freezer, her hands automatically reaching for the coffee she couldn't live without, and wondered again what on earth she was thinking by not flat out saying no to Nick's outrageous proposition of sex lessons.

Then she remembered her dream. Despite how dumb it might be to mix her friendship with sex, she was probably going to end up saying yes.

Searching for her favorite coffee cup and finding it in the sink, dirty, Lacey cringed. "Lord, I seriously need to get a grip on my lazy housekeeping ways."

As she started washing the pink mug that read, "Don't like my attitude? Send me an email at: like_I_Care@fu.com", Lacey couldn't help laughing at the irony of her situation.

"A personal trainer, needing a very personal trainer. How nuts is that?"

All joking aside, the truth was still there staring her in the face like a black cloud. She did need help in the bedroom. Lacey was obviously too boring to hold a man's attention. Evan was the perfect example.

If Nick was anything in real life like he was in her dream world then she was certain to end up a virtuoso in the fine art of sex.

Nick hung up the phone, got out of bed and headed toward the bathroom. He stripped out of his boxers and turned on the shower. Only when he could feel the hot water sluicing down his back did he indulge in thoughts of Lacey.

He loved knocking her off balance. She was floundering in

her safe, little world and they both knew it. There was no way he'd let her escape him this time. She was almost within reach, and after their workout she would be all his. About damn time, too. He was going insane wanting her.

After yet another restless night of dreaming of Lacey's sleek, strong legs, small, firm breasts and heart-shaped ass, Nick couldn't have kept himself from reaching for the phone if he'd been hogtied. It had been vital to hear her husky morning voice.

She'd sounded groggy, but when she'd heard his voice, her attitude had shifted, becoming instantly alert and on guard. He could tell she'd lied about sleeping soundly. If she were any other woman, he would have called her out on it. Made her admit his heated words and touches the night before had aroused her. He wasn't a complete moron when it came to women. He knew arousal when he saw it. Or heard it.

Had she dreamed of him? Nick was almost sure of it. Had she gotten hot thinking of what he might soon be doing to her? He could only hope. He wanted her turned on and anxious. Served her right for making him so crazy.

Nick finished his shower, got dressed and drove to the office. Surprisingly his vehicle wasn't the only one there. As he was about to get on the elevator he ran into Merrick. Nick let the elevator go and turned his attention to his friend. "What brings you in? I didn't think anything could pry you out of Chloe's warm arms on a lazy Saturday morning."

Merrick shoved his hands into his jean pockets. "Probably same as you. I wanted to take one last look at the Cooper account."

Nick laughed. That was one of the things he admired about Merrick Vaughn. He worked as hard as anyone else. Just because he was the owner and CEO of Vaughn Business

Solutions didn't mean he was willing to leave the day-to-day running of the business to his employees.

"Yep, same reason I'm here. I wanted to be fresh on Monday."

"I tried calling you last night, got voicemail instead. Were you out with a woman?"

Nick shrugged. "I took Lacey to a movie. She was feeling down about Evan."

Merrick's face turned hard. "Yeah, I heard. What a dick. I'd like to kick his damned teeth in, personally. But that would only piss off Lacey."

Nick leaned against the wall next to the elevator and fiddled with his keys. He still hated to think about Evan and Lacey together. It set him on edge.

"My thoughts exactly. It put a dent in your sister's self-esteem a little," Nick admitted.

Merrick stared at him for a long minute, as if weighing his next words very carefully. "She told you that?"

Nick nodded, unsure about Merrick's subdued attitude. He was always easy going with him, but this particular conversation made Nick increasingly aware that Merrick was about to say something he wasn't going to like.

"Yeah. I think it messed with her quite a bit because she thought Christy was her friend."

"Makes sense," Merrick said. In a quieter tone he asked, "So, what time did you get home last night?"

Nick quirked a brow at Merrick and posed a question of his own, "You keeping tabs?"

Merrick's eyes narrowed and his jaw firmed. "What you do with your time is your business, but what you do with my sister is my business."

Did Merrick know how completely archaic that sounded? Then again, if he had a sister he would probably be the same way, whether she was grown woman or not. However, Merrick should know Lacey wasn't a weakling in need of saving.

"She's all grown up, Merrick. She can take care of herself, don't you think?"

"No. I don't." Merrick stepped closer until they were eye to eye. "The rules change where Lacey's concerned. She's not just some woman. She's my baby sister. She's Blade's baby sister."

Merrick just had to bring up the eldest and most forbidding of the Vaughn brothers. Shit. Nick hadn't considered the two Vaughn men breathing down his neck when he'd embarked on his "Seduce Lacey" campaign.

Nick shoved a hand through his hair and tried to be as honest as possible without revealing too much. "I care about her, damn it. I'd never do anything to hurt her. I give you my word."

Merrick stood there for another minute, a blazing intensity in his eyes as he silently sized him up. Finally he nodded, and even smiled before stating. "Good enough for me."

Nick started to breathe again. It would surely put a crimp in his relationship with Lacey if he was forced into a brawl with one—or both—of her brothers.

"But, it may not be good enough for Blade," Merrick said. "He's a little more old-fashioned than I am. As far as he's concerned, Lacey is made of fine crystal and should be treated accordingly. He's not a man you want as an enemy. He's already called Evan and put the fear of God into him. Think about that before you do anything stupid, like make Lacey sad. Or worse, make Lacey sad in front of Blade."

Nick was six-foot two and two hundred pounds of adult male muscle. He could take down most any man.

Compelled to come to his own defense, as well as Lacey's, he stated, "Thanks for the advice, but you both need to remember Lacey is a woman with a mind of her own. If she wants something, no amount of intimidation will stop her. And you also need to keep in mind that while I do respect Lacey's family, what goes on between us is private business. No one else's."

Merrick nodded. "I can understand that. But you'd be wise not to hurt her."

Thank God, Merrick looked like he was leaving. Nick was fast running out of things to say. In all his dating experience, he'd never once been forced to deal with over-protective brothers. It was bizarre, to say the least.

They agreed to meet later at Merrick's house for a game of basketball then parted ways. Nick pushed the elevator button again. The doors opened and he stepped inside. As they closed again, sealing him in and the rest of the world out, he turned his thoughts inward.

It was funny to hear Merrick talk of Lacey as if she were a schoolgirl. He'd never had a sister, only one brother, and they weren't all that close. Jonathon was a good guy, a hard worker and only two years his junior, but they weren't raised like the Vaughn family.

In the Stone household, life was quiet and dull. There were no big family get-togethers, and he could count on one hand the amount of times he'd received a hug from either of his parents. After he'd graduated from high school, it was a given that he'd go to college. That's when his life had really begun. He'd proven he could make it on his own, be his own man.

He loved his family, but the cold, sterile life they led wasn't for him. Nick was the black sheep, simply because he wanted a family who would welcome him home from work with a kiss and a smile. He wanted kids. He wanted to go on family vacations. He wanted to celebrate everything from a good grade to his child's college graduation. Because of his views, Nick rarely spoke to or saw his family. They found him peculiar. Which was appropriate, since he'd always seen them in the same light.

When the elevator stopped, he stepped out and went to his office. His last thought before setting his mind to business was how perfect it'd be if he had all those things with Lacey. For the first time since he'd started seeing her as more than a friend, Nick felt like maybe, just maybe that dream wasn't so implausible anymore.

Chapter Four

"Nick, as in your best friend, Nick?" Patty asked incredulously.

"The very same," Lacey answered as she finished off her second glass of diet cola and dug into her salad.

Her friends Patty Baronette and Mary Riser both stared at her as if she'd lost her mind.

"Well, what did you tell him?" Mary asked, looking completely shocked by the idea that any man would suggest sex lessons.

"I told him I needed time to think about it." Lacey dropped that bomb then dug back into her salad.

Patty laughed while Mary glanced around, as if afraid someone might hear their sinful conversation. "I can't believe you're even considering his offer," Mary said, as if she were sixty instead of twenty-three.

"I think I'm going to accept." *There, take that,* Lacey thought. She was so damn tired of Mary's self-righteous attitude. It grated on her last nerve. She always looked at her as if she was some dirty little tramp. As if she needed to personally stitch a scarlet A across Lacey's sweater to warn unsuspecting men. Why Lacey stayed friends with her was a mystery. She supposed it was partly because Mary had been part of their little group right from the beginning. And while she did get annoying at times, she still had some redeeming qualities, all of which Lacey was having a hard time remembering at the moment.

"Well, I for one am all for it," Patty stated. "Hell, Nick is one delicious-looking man. If I wasn't already so in love with Ralph and Nick had offered to give me sex lessons, you can bet your britches I'd jump on the offer. No pun intended, of course."

Mary turned beet red, and Lacey chuckled. Patty laughed, too, and finally Mary offered a slight snicker.

Lacey looked at her watch and sobered when she saw the time. In thirty minutes she would need to give Nick her answer. "Oh God, what if this screws everything up? I couldn't live with it, you guys. He's been there for me through so much, and I just don't know what I'd do without him."

Mary looked at her with thoughtful eyes. "You know, he has been there for you, and you've been there for him. Has it ever occurred to either of you that maybe you guys are already halfway to being a couple?"

Lacey dropped her fork. Patty swung her gaze toward Mary then back to Lacey. No way could she prevent the heat from searing her cheeks.

"You are way off there, Mary. We're just friends. Nick is just doing me a favor, there's nothing more to it. I know it."

Mary shrugged, but Patty frowned. "If it were me, I'd want that confirmed."

"What do you mean?"

"Lay it all on the table. Make him tell you he's only helping you before you slip between the sheets."

Lacey nodded vehemently. "Yeah, good idea."

"And don't go into this thing thinking he's only doing you a favor, hon," Patty continued. "If he's offering up his...services, you can bet he's thought about this before. Probably more than once."

Lacey licked her lips nervously, willing the waiter to bring her another diet cola—her version of liquid courage. "He said as much."

Patty and Mary both leaned close. Patty asked, "Come again?"

Lacey tried to act nonchalant, as if they were talking about the weather, clothes, books, anything but sex with Nick Stone. It wasn't an easy sham to pull off.

"He said he wanted me. That he wasn't just doing me a favor, because he wants me naked, in bed, and all his."

"Damn. That's hot," Patty groaned, as she began to fan her face. "That's just so damn hot."

Mary started fidgeting, as if the conversation was making her a little bit warm too. Hmm, maybe Mary wasn't quite the goody-goody she always acted.

"Well, I'm not sure how this thing will play out, but I do need work on my...bedroom skills, or else Evan wouldn't have bothered with Christy."

Patty waved the words away. "That's just crap. Evan was a weasel, and you deserve better. Period."

"Evan was always eyeing Christy. I never did much care for her. She seemed to enjoy the way he stared at her. If she were a true friend, she would have told him to go suck an egg." Mary's words in her defense surprised Lacey.

Wow. That was the thing about Mary. Just when Lacey thought she had her friend figured out, she went and mixed it up again.

The three of them had met at the gym. Both women had come in looking to shed a few pounds and they'd hit it off. They weren't clients of hers personally. Neither of the women made the kind of money that would afford them a personal trainer. Even though Lacey had offered them both a personal discount, they still declined, stating they were too lazy for that kind of commitment. Two years had gone by and they were still close friends.

While she knew a great deal about Patty's life, she knew very little about Mary's. Patty worked at a local grocery store and was happily engaged to a wonderful man. They wanted to get married in the fall and start right away on having kids. Mary lived alone. She worked as a Chiropractic Assistant, and from what Lacey could see she didn't date much. She'd often tried to get her to open up, come out of her shell, but it never seemed to work. Mary had been raised in an extremely strict household, with sickeningly rigid parents. She never offered any other information. She supposed, given the way Mary grew up, she should cut her some slack, but sometimes her I'm-better-than-you attitude wore on Lacey's nerves. Depressing background or not.

Lacey's diet cola finally arrived. "Oh, bless you." She told the waiter. The guy gave her a wide smile and sauntered off. She sucked it down, glad to have at least that much to get her through the rest of the day. She had a feeling she'd need to stay alert and ready. Nick could be seriously persistent and extremely cunning when it came to a woman he wanted. She'd seen him in action with other women and she still wasn't sure if the shiver running up her spine now was from fear or excitement.

"Damn, woman, are you trying to kill me?"

"What's the matter, Nick? Am I too much woman for you?"

"Not a chance, baby. You and I are a perfect fit." His voice

53

dropped an octave as he leaned toward her to whisper, "You'll soon see just how perfect."

"Nick," Lacey groused, "focus, damn it."

They'd been working out for only half an hour and she was having the hardest time keeping his mind off her and on their exercise routine. Now, as they did crunches side by side, he kept looking over at her, groaning and saying completely inappropriate things. It obliterated her concentration, and she was growing increasingly warm. Unfortunately, the burn had nothing to do with their workout and everything to do with Nick.

"Oh believe me, I'm totally focused."

"Nick," she said in warning.

He placed his palm to her lower abs. The movement thrust Lacey back into her dream as she remembered him doing the very same thing while they made love. She dropped down onto the floor and looked at him. "What are you doing?"

"You promised an answer for me. I've yet to receive one."

"Will you let me finish working out first?"

"I don't think I can stand the suspense. Please, I need to know if you're willing to let me help you get over this silly fear you have of being an inadequate lover."

"Yes!" Lacey blurted.

"Yes?" Nick's voice sounded harsh, as if raked over hot coals.

"Yes. I want you to...instruct me," she explained, her stomach clenching tight.

"Fuck, Lacey."

Nick's hand began to massage her stomach, and she nearly forgot where they were. She quickly put her palm over his, stopping his actions. "We're in a gym full of people here."

Nick looked around them then back at her, a cocky grin on his handsome face. "Everyone else is in the main area, baby. We're all alone back here in your little private workout room."

"We need to finish exercising. Don't we?" All of a sudden, she wasn't so sure. His hand had drifted downward and it cupped her mound through her black workout shorts.

"We'll get a workout, don't worry. For now, I just want to touch you. May I?"

"Yes," she said breathlessly. "I suppose that wouldn't be too bad."

The carnal expression that spread across Nick's face wasn't at all reassuring. The little lopsided tilt to his sensual lips gave her body an inner jolt, which went clear to her toes. Nick was so clever in his movements, too, and Lacey had the feeling he would be the most adept man when it came to foreplay. As his mouth skimmed below her ear, touching a particularly sensitive spot, she became aware of one other thing. She really didn't want to think too much about how he'd come by such expertise. *Enjoy and learn,* she reminded herself. This was only the first in many such moments. Once Nick was through with her, Lacey would have the confidence to get any man she wanted.

Which was exactly why they were doing this.

If that were the case then why was she so easily imagining Nick making love to her, as opposed to what he would really be doing, which was teaching her? Helping her get over some insecurities. Lovemaking didn't have anything to do with it.

That was a given.

Her thoughts scattered to the farthest corners of the earth as Nick's fingers found their way beneath her shorts. "Damn, I can't believe I'm touching lace."

"I'm wearing cotton," she mumbled.

"Mmm, yes you are."

Then his fingers moved past her panties as he stroked the curls of her mound. It was such a forbidden thing for Lacey, making out in her place of business. She always left her feminine side outside the gym. Here she was a personal trainer. She helped men and women alike learn to live a healthy lifestyle. Only now, all she saw was Nick. All she felt was his overheated skin, his breath against her neck. All she smelled was the potent mixture of sweat and man and desire. She was more aroused than she'd ever been, and he hadn't done a single thing but touch.

"Nick, please," Lacey found herself pleading.

Nick leaned over her until he was staring directly into her half-closed eyes and growled, "Please what, baby?" He skimmed his thumb over her clitoris and asked teasingly, "Please do this?"

She wanted to speak, really she did, but his touch was electric. Lacey was a marionette, and only Nick had the power to make her come alive.

Then his finger dipped between her nether lips and she lost control. She pushed into his hand, seeking more, wanting him so deep he could never find his way free again.

"You like that, don't you?" he whispered against her lips as he kissed her. "Would you like two fingers even more?"

Lacey nodded, beyond caring where she was, beyond caring about her own name even.

"No. Tell me you want two fingers inside this hot little cunt. Give it to me, baby."

"Yes, Nick, two. And please don't stop."

His smile fluttered against her cheek. She felt his triumph. It radiated off him in masculine waves. Any other time and she'd be tossing out a sarcastic, witty reply to such arrogance. Not this time. All she wanted was Nick and the things only he could make her feel.

Intense, hot, eager. She'd never been like that with a man. Yet, a few touches, a few strokes from Nick and she was on fire, ready to hand him her body on a silver platter. It was frightening and exciting at once.

He stroked her inner flesh, all the while flicking back and forth over her clit. With no warning, her body rocketed out of control. Nick was right there, drinking in her moans of pleasure. With his mouth against hers, he masked her wild sounds and gave her the climax of a lifetime.

A few heavy breaths later, Nick slowly pulled his wet fingers from between her legs. He brought them to his mouth and slid both between his lips. He kept his gaze locked with hers as he fed off her juices, swallowing every drop.

"Remember the time, right after you and Dick broke up, we were sitting on your living room couch and you were laughing over the way Dick used to want to turn the lights off every time you two made love?"

Where had that come from? She could barely breathe, her body was still vibrating, and he wanted to talk about past lovers?

"Uh, yeah, I remember. But his name was Richard, not Dick."

"Whatever. Anyway, you were sprawled out on the couch, your foot in my lap. I was massaging it, and all I could think was how soft your pussy must be under those tight gray shorts you wore." He looked down her body as if reliving that day all over again then ground out, "God, I wanted so badly to reach down and finger-fuck you. You have no clue how hard it was to control myself, baby. No idea."

Lacey was floored. Could it be true? Did Nick find her sexy? How could she not have known? Lacey lifted up to a sitting position and watched as Nick's intense gaze tracked her every move, as if worried she might slip away if he so much as blinked. She looked him over from head to toe, enthralled all over again by what a perfect body he had. He was so hard, so big and so...hers. But it wasn't just that. Lacey knew Nick inside and out and he was the best sort of man. He ranked right up there with her brothers, which was saying something. Only she didn't feel the least bit sisterly with Nick. Then again, if she knew him so well, why hadn't she known he was attracted to her? That he'd wanted her?

"Why didn't you ever say anything? Why, Nick?" The question had been on the tip of her tongue each time he'd shared another tidbit with her. He reclined on the floor, flat on his back, his head resting on his folded arms. Lacey couldn't look away. His deep brown eyes mesmerized her. Had he always had that mysterious intensity and she just hadn't noticed?

"Because you would've freaked."

Lacey shook her head, vehemently denying it. "No, I wouldn't."

Nick reached a hand up and cupped her cheek. "Be honest with yourself, Lace. You never saw me as anything more than a friend. If I started telling you how sexy you were, that I wanted to get naked with you and do the freaky horizontal, you would have gone running for the hills."

"The freaky horizontal?" Lacey choked out around a laugh.

Nick's face split into a grin. "Or the freaky vertical, I'm cool with that, too."

Lacey laughed full-out. "Lord, help me. What have I gotten myself into?"

Chapter Five

After her orgasmic afternoon delight, they'd separated to the locker rooms and taken showers. They were now in his driveway and Lacey was nervously chatting about a client who hadn't lost any weight. Nick half-listened as he stared at his front porch.

Lacey had been to his home before, lots of times, but only as a friend. Never as his lover. Everything took on new meaning now.

His house could have been right out of a home decorating magazine. Nestled in a suburb of Columbus, Ohio, it was incredibly homey. He could easily visualize a couple of rowdy kids playing h-o-r-s-e. He was all set for a family; he only needed the wife to get things started. Not just any wife would do. He wanted Lacey.

"Nick, I just have one more question."

"Shoot, baby." He was so far gone at this point he'd tell her anything to get her inside the house and away from prying eyes. Nick loved his neighbors, but they could be damn nosy at times.

Lacey squinted at him suspiciously. "This thing between us, is it just sex lessons?"

Lacey seemed to be holding her breath, as if terrified he was going to say it was much more. He studiously ignored the part of his soul that was afraid she'd never see him as anything more than a means to an end. If he were completely honest with himself, of all the things Nick thought she'd ask, this was nowhere on the list.

"You're thinking it death. It'll all work out, I promise." he hedged.

She visibly relaxed, but Nick could practically see her walls going back up. What had she been hoping he'd say? He mentally stored the question away for later. Right now, he wanted to kick off his newest venture as Lacey's sex instructor.

"Come on, baby, quit stalling." He opened his door and left the car, pleased when she did the same. He started to make his way around the hood to take her hand when Lacey stopped him. "I just thought of something. I don't have anything with me. We should have stopped at my apartment first."

He knew she was nervous, otherwise she would've remembered her stash of clothes and toiletries. She'd stayed over before. Once when she'd had too much to drink, which for Lacey was all of two beers. Also, a couple of times when a movie they watched ran late and he wouldn't let her leave—for safety reasons, he'd told her. The truth was, he liked having her in his home. Nick enjoyed waking up and finding her all curled up in his bed, looking adorable as hell. So much so that he hadn't minded sleeping on the couch.

In two long strides, he was in front of her, taking her hand and murmuring, "Remember when you slept over that night last year? It was New Year's Eve and you'd gotten a little tipsy. I had to put you to bed."

She nodded, smiling up at him with a mixture of woman and friend. It drove him crazy every time. "Didn't you ever wonder how you ended up in my t-shirt the next morning?"

Lacey blushed. Every time her cheeks filled with color it turned him on. Lacey's blush was more potent than another woman's touch.

"I didn't even think about it, because—"

"Because you hardly remember anything when you drink. You thought you'd changed into the shirt yourself and just didn't remember doing it." She nodded again. "You didn't. I undressed you and put you to bed that night."

"Oh God."

"Don't go all shy on me, baby. I made a point of getting the job done as quickly as I could. Still, I did see you in your underwear. You'd just gotten out from under the clutches of Lucas the Octopus and you were feeling sort of low that night."

"I remember. I didn't particularly miss Lucas, but I was feeling crappy thinking another year was gone and I was still no closer to finding my Mr. Right."

"Yeah, you told me that. Lacey, did you never wonder why I wasn't with anyone that night either?"

He could see the chagrin come over her face and she started to stammer. He stopped her with a finger to her lips.

"I wasn't with anyone because I knew you were alone and all I could think about was maybe this time Lacey Vaughn would see me as a man, and not just a good pal."

"Oh."

Nick went back to the question she'd originally asked. "You don't need anything from your apartment for what I have in mind. This time, I won't be quick when I undress you, either. This time I'm going to take it real slow, and I'm going to take a long time looking."

He watched, mesmerized, as she licked her lips. The way her nipples went perky and her breathing sped up made him want to jump her right there in his driveway. Push her against his SUV and fuck her from behind.

Unable to help himself any longer, Nick lowered his head and touched his mouth to hers, kissing her with a gentleness which surprised even him. The warm summer night, full moon high in the sky, and Lacey's soft full lips pressed against his. Oh yeah, Nick could easily believe in all that magic Lacey had talked about the night before.

He kept the kiss brief, all too aware they were out in the open. When he raised his head, he saw her half-closed eyes and knew his control would snap if she so much as whimpered. Having her against his SUV wasn't exactly a bad idea, but it wasn't what he wanted for Lacey's first time with him either.

Nick touched her moist, plump lips with his index finger and whispered, "Trust me?" She nodded, making him feel ten feet tall. He turned, keeping her hand in his, and strode up to the front door.

Feeling pumped, he just barely managed to get his door unlocked. Inside, the house was dark and empty. God, he hated it. This time, however, he had Lacey with him, and he wouldn't let her go. Not without a fight. And she would fight him.

Lacey ran from love. Her fear of commitment was the reason behind all the failed relationships. He didn't know if it was because some asshole had crushed her heart at one time, or if there was something deeper. Either way, he would make her see that love could be a beautiful and exciting adventure. A thing to cherish and nurture. Not something to hide from in fright.

First, Nick had to get her to open up to him, to give herself to him one small piece at a time. The way she'd opened up to him at the gym was a good start. He knew enough about Lacey to know she would never do something so outrageous at her place of business. She took pride in her work as a personal trainer. The very fact that he was able to make her forget herself, for even a few moments, was a good sign. She needed to trust him with her body completely. Later he would show her she could trust him with her heart.

Nick let go of her hand and moved to flip on the lamp beside the couch. When he turned back around, he was struck speechless. She was so damned sweet.

Standing all of about five foot one, Lacey gave off a fragile appearance. Men wanted to protect and shelter her. But she packed a punch. Literally. She was in excellent physical condition and believed wholeheartedly in practicing what she preached. Exercise and nutrition was Lacey's life and she had a huge clientele as evidence that she was good at her job.

While she was slender and fit, her curves were still lush and inviting. She had small, tantalizing breasts that he'd fantasized about. What shade of pink were her nipples? Were they dark mauve or pale pink? Soon he'd know.

Truthfully, it had been her ass that had hooked him from almost the very beginning. She had a nice firm backside that made his mouth water every time he looked at it. Which was often.

Her hair was cut just below her shoulders out of necessity. She always worked up a sweat at the gym and showering twice, sometimes three times a day, meant she needed to keep it at a reasonable length. The pin-straight, rich espresso color tempted a man to dig his fingers in and play. And it was way past time for Nick to have a little fun.

Lacey stood just inside the front door, so rigid and nervous, as if about to bolt at any moment. Her anxiety insured a slow plan of action. She was still getting used to the idea of being with him intimately, where as he'd thought of nothing else for months. He didn't need time to consider what happens after, because he already knew. Once he made her his, there would be no going back. She just wasn't aware of that fact. Yet.

With that thought in mind, Nick gave Lacey a flirtatious grin and crooked a finger at her. "Come over here." Her blue eyes grew big and her mouth opened as if she were about to refuse him. "You ready for your second lesson?" he prompted.

Her mouth snapped shut and his eyes were inexorably drawn once more to her breasts where her nipples pushed sensually against her t-shirt. Nick's cock swelled in response. God, how he wanted to taste her. To feel her soft skin against his lips, his tongue. He had to tamp down the urge to take her where she stood.

Lacey had never seen this side of Nick, and she couldn't believe she was seeing it now. She'd been around aroused men before, but never were they so...hot and impatient. She was beginning to think giving her lessons was only a convenient way for him to get what he wanted. Her. He had said as much, but the notion still made her want to backpedal.

Nick continued to wait. His charming smile entranced her. Lacey's stomach fluttered with nerves. She was eager, but tense, too. Was she really about to indulge in a no-strings attached affair? It was crazy. She'd never done crazy. Any woman would be nervous. Her choice of lovers was definitely the right one, though.

Nick was tall, gorgeous and honorable. She wouldn't have to worry about him becoming too possessive. They were already friends, and if things started to turn stale, they could go back to being friends. She could then use all her new knowledge on someone else.

Why didn't that last thought sound very appealing?

If there was one thing Lacey knew about Nick, it was that he would always be straight with her. He was honest to the point of being obnoxious at times. The idea was to teach her a few things about sex and he had been candid when he'd admitted he was sexually attracted to her. A new sense of freedom came over her as she made up her mind. For tonight, she was going to quit worrying and let loose a little. What would it hurt?

Lacey stepped away from the safety of the front door and let Nick take her in his embrace. When his powerful arms closed around her, she saw the triumphant gleam in his chocolate eyes.

"Feeling pretty darn sure of yourself aren't you?" she taunted.

The low rumble of his voice vibrated against her ear as he answered her. "I have the sexy Lacey Vaughn all to myself. Damn right I feel confident."

The man was too cocky. It was high time someone knocked Nick Stone down a peg or two. Perhaps she was just the woman for the job.

Nick pulled her tighter against him. Tilting up her head, he took her mouth in a hard show of possession. His tongue darted out and licked at the seam of her lips, all but demanding she open for him. Lacey had no choice but to obey. As soon as her lips parted, he took advantage and delved in.

His hands were everywhere. They slid down her back to her bottom where he cupped her close and pulled her into the cradle of his thighs. She groaned, or he did, she wasn't sure. All that mattered was that he continue kissing her. Lacey was on fire. Her entire body responded to the feel of his lean strength against her giving flesh.

Nick tilted his head and she raised her hands to grasp the sides of his neck, holding him to her. She tunneled her fingers through the dark strands of his hair, reveling in its softness.

His tongue touched and played with hers, darting in and out, mimicking lovemaking. He was hungry. Urgent. Challenging. Lacey couldn't stand it anymore.

Pulling back, breathing as if she'd run four laps around the gym, Lacey moaned, "Bedroom, now."

She turned and started in that direction, but a hand at the back of her waistband pulled her up short.

"Not quite yet," Nick ground out.

Lacey stared, confused and anxious. "Huh?"

"Lesson two, remember?" he reminded her.

"Yeah, lesson two. You can tell me all about it in the bedroom." Lacey tugged on his hand again and smiled up at him. He looked so sweet, so ravenous, as if he were drinking her in with his eyes. It was the ultimate temptation.

"No," he said, attempting to sound stern. He failed miserably, because Lacey wasn't buying it.

She was about to push a little more, but he placed his index finger to her lips and murmured, "We need to slow down a little, baby."

She pouted, but Nick only closed his eyes. Darn it. She was getting nowhere fast.

Lacey moved his finger and protested, "I don't see why. Things are going pretty well at this pace."

Nick opened his eyes and stared at the woman before him. She was begging him for sex. What the hell was his problem? Easy. He wanted this to be about more than lessons. Regardless of what he'd told her, he knew if they went into the bedroom, it'd be wham, bam, and she'd be walking right out of his life. No fucking way.

"If we don't slow down I'm going to come way before you

ever get a hint of pleasure. I've waited too long for this already." He watched her gaze flit down his body as if trying to see right through the fabric of his jeans. She was such an inferno of needs and wants right now, and that was as it should be, but Nick wanted more than Lacey's body. He wanted an emotional intimacy with her and he couldn't get that if he let her have her way.

Nick touched the tip of her nose and smiled. "First we get to know each other. That's lesson two. Learning to appreciate the moment."

Lacey rolled her eyes at him. "I *am* appreciating the moment. Besides, we already know each other."

"Not in the way of lovers we don't. We know each other as buddies. That's not the same thing. Not by a long shot."

She looked dubious. "Well yeah, that's sort of what I was trying to do, get to know you as a lover."

Nick had no idea restraint could be so difficult. She was just so damned tempting. But he wouldn't be a substitute for cookies. Right now that's all it would be for Lacey. A way to drown her problems in a few blissful moments of sensual gratification.

He rubbed his hand over his face, trying to gather his fortitude. "Lacey, I want to spend time with you. I want to touch and cuddle. Ease into the moment, ya know?"

Lacey sighed. "It occurs to me that I am way out of my element with you, Nick. I don't know what you want from me. Most men are perfectly content keeping it simple. First sex then get to know each other. I seem to be a virgin at real intimacy." She let out a sigh, as if accepting the inevitable. "You win. What do you suggest?"

Thank you, God! If she had put up even one more protest Nick would have given in and done things her way. He had a feeling that would be a huge mistake.

"While I desperately want to take you into the bedroom and make love to you all night long, in as many different ways as I can possibly imagine, I think we need to slow down. Just a little."

Lacey seemed to relax and even grinned.

"It's a mild, clear night outside. Feel like sitting on the porch with me?" He could see her nervousness still, so he softly added, "No expectations. Just me, you and the stars."

"Lead the way, Casanova." She thrust out her hand, appeared pleased when he took it and let him take her to the front porch. Right away Nick felt the connection between them growing stronger. She was more relaxed than he'd ever seen her. This would be nice, he decided. This is what she needed from a man. Not just wild and crazy sex, but a real bond.

They would cuddle and talk about nothing in particular, and then when the time was right, they'd head back into the house and he would take her to his bed where she belonged.

Chapter Six

She was so embarrassed. Lacey couldn't believe she'd actually fallen asleep. Never had she done something so rude. It was mortifying.

On a happy note, she'd had the best night's sleep in a long time. But would Nick ever forgive her? The last thing she remembered was sitting on the porch swing with Nick making wishes under the stars. It had been comfortable. Right. Then she woke up in his bed, with her jeans and t-shirt still on, no shoes, tucked under the covers. Had Nick actually carried her to bed while she'd snoozed? She couldn't believe she'd slept through something so wonderful.

"Life is so not fair," Lacey grumbled as she rolled out of bed, hastily shed her clothes and hopped into Nick's shower. She wanted to find him and apologize properly for being so terribly rude. With any luck, he'd give her another chance.

Ten minutes later, she stepped out of the shower and dried off using one of his oversized towels. She pressed her nose to the terrycloth and inhaled. Was it her imagination or could she really smell him? She slipped into a pair of jean shorts and a black crop top that she'd left at his place before then left the room. She didn't bother to fix her hair; it would just have to dry naturally.

Moving down the hallway, she was caught by the sound of

snoring. Nick always snored ridiculously loud. She looked toward the couch and there he lay, sprawled out. No shirt, no shoes, nothing but his jeans with the top button undone. Lord have mercy, the man had a fine looking chest and abs.

Tufts of soft, dark hair curled around each nipple and trailed a path downward over a taut stomach, only to disappear into the waistband of his jeans. His jaw was unshaven. If it were possible, he looked even more gorgeous. Sort of rougher around the edges. She had a moment to wonder what he'd look like with a mustache. Hmm, very handsome, probably. The man looked sinful no matter what.

Lacey tiptoed over to the coffee table directly across from the couch and sat. She touched his jaw. He had such strong, masculine features. She traced one finger down his face to his collarbone and his chest. She had the overpowering urge to lick his nipples.

But her finger had a mind of its own as it continued to travel down his perfect body only to trace the button on his pants. Just as she started to reluctantly pull her hand away, Lacey heard a gravelly voice say, "Don't stop now, I was just beginning to enjoy myself."

She thrust backward as if burned. "Uh, sorry. I was just, um, well, I was..." What could she say? Uh gee I was just molesting you in your sleep. No biggie.

"I was only trying to wake you."

"I could really get use to that kind of wake up call."

He had a lethal glint in his dark fathomless eyes. One she'd never seen before, and it prompted her into action. "Well, now that you're up, I wanted to tell you how sorry I was for falling asleep on you last night. It was rude and unforgivable." She started to get up, but his hand snaked out and grabbed her arm, holding her in place.

"You have no idea how up I am," he growled. "And I never did get my good night kiss. You owe me, Lace, and now I'm collecting." He pulled her off the table and on top of him then crushed his mouth to hers.

It was a hard, brutal kiss, not at all gentle. Nick was hot and insistent. Something inside of her responded to his primitive demand. She didn't want it to end. Yet, at the same time, she needed it to stop..

His lips stayed hard against hers, and the feel of him beneath her had her losing reason. Lacey wanted him to take her. She wanted to please him. To do everything he wished and fulfill all his fantasies.

Last night, Nick had relished taking Lacey to bed, tucking her in and letting her dream deeply. This morning, he was beyond ready to get inside her tight body. Now was the time for him to get a taste of what had been out of his reach for far too long.

Nick wanted to seduce her into submitting to him. He could, and he knew it. He needed to take the lead. To show her how perfect it could be. How perfect he knew it would be, because everything about Lacey was perfect.

She was what a man desired in a woman. Soft, womanly curves, a sweet innocence that made him want to shelter and protect, and a hot, steamy inner passion just begging to be released. She was so ripe. Nick ached to pluck her from the vine that kept her chained and taste every juicy inch.

Lacey whimpered and went pliant in his arms. It was all the encouragement he needed. If Nick couldn't have all of her today, right now then he'd at least take a sample. Something that would stick with him, tide him over until he could have it all.

He used his tongue to coax her lips apart, licking at the

delicate skin until she finally surrendered. He entered the sweet cavern of her mouth and explored its wet heat. He moved his tongue in a rhythm akin to making love, going slowly in and out, building the pleasure by small measures. Suddenly, Lacey's delicate hands were in his hair. She grabbed handfuls and pulled him closer still.

Nick took his mouth from hers. "Baby, I want you. I want to be buried inside of you until you scream my name. God, how I've fantasized about that." He shut his eyes for a minute in an effort to gain control before opening them again. "But I'm not sure you're ready." When she started to protest, he hushed her by placing his index finger to her lips. "I will give you an appetizer." No way was he going to leave her wanting.

Nick turned them so she lay against the couch, his body covering hers. He touched his tongue to her lips again, but this time it was just a bare whisper. Even so, Lacey whimpered again. The teasing little sound could be addicting.

He kissed each of her eyelids and trailed his lips along her cheeks, taking his time, drawing out the pleasure. If only it would last forever. Every time she blinked, every time she moved, he wanted her to think only of him and beg him for more.

Sitting back on his haunches, he pulled her top up over her head, and threw it on the floor. She wasn't wearing a bra and his eyes drank in her delicate form. Baby-pink. That was the shade of her nipples. They were large and puffy. He'd never seen anything sweeter, or more tempting.

"Oh, baby, you are every man's fantasy come to life, and you're all mine."

Not giving her a chance to respond, he leaned down and sucked one pink tip into his mouth, rolling it with his tongue and biting it lightly, giving in to the frantic need clawing at him.

He closed his eyes and savored her unique flavor.

One last lick and he released the hard bud then pulled back to gaze into her eyes. "You taste as good as you smell. Somehow I knew you would." His voice was almost unrecognizable even to him. He descended onto the other breast, brushing it with his tongue while his hand was busy toying and kneading the other.

"Nick, please, I want you."

It was almost too much. He stopped his ministrations and taunted, "Good, I want you crazy for it, Lace." Then he crawled down her body, and undid the fly to her jean shorts. He slithered them down her strong, runner's legs, kissing each inch of flesh he exposed. He stopped in surprise when he got her shorts off all the way and looked at her panties. "Christ, had I known what you were wearing I would have moved a hell of a lot faster."

She wore a lacey turquoise thong. Nick could clearly see her brown curls underneath the scarce covering. The beautiful sight fired his blood.

It made him so hard he ached.

"Did I ever tell you that turquoise is my favorite color?" he asked, his eyes never leaving her nest of curls. When he thought he heard a whispered "no", he groaned, "Well it sure as hell is now."

With her shorts all the way off, he looked down at her. Passion darkened her pale blue eyes and her face was rosy from the scrape of his morning stubble. Her damp, silky hair fanned out across the cushion. He had a moment to think of just how sexy she appeared. His gaze darted to her nipples, distended and wet from his loving. He rumbled his approval and fondled the firm globes. He'd waited for this moment far too long and yet it was better than he'd ever imagined. He felt like a kid with a new toy.

Lacey brought up her hands in a modest attempt to cover her body from his view. He wouldn't let her hide. Nick clutched her wrists in one of his fists then raised them above her head. She was totally exposed to him. Vulnerable and submissive. His dick throbbed.

"Don't ever cover yourself from me," he ordered. "I won't have you feeling embarrassed. Remember lesson one?"

She nodded.

"Mmm, good girl."

He lowered his head and kissed the wetness between her thighs. He sucked her tiny nub into his mouth, panties and all. Lacey went wild beneath him. It was so damn erotic to suck on her swollen clit through lace.

She tried to pry her hands free, but Nick wouldn't let her. He held her still and continued to keep her restrained while he teased and stroked her to a fever pitch. All at once, she moaned his name and pushed her pussy into his eager mouth as her climax washed over her.

While she continued to pulse and arch into him, Nick knew it was the first time he'd tasted heaven. At Lacey's wild response, he had to wonder how long it'd been since she'd had an orgasm. Hadn't Evan considered Lacey's pleasure over his own? Probably not, the selfish prick. He could kill Evan. Still, Nick was glad to be the man to make her come so completely undone now. He'd never heard a more beautiful sound.

When her spasms subsided, he demanded, "Open your pretty eyes, Lace." When she obeyed, his voice turned as hard as steel. "You're mine now." He licked her clit once more, sealing the deal. "Every delicious inch of you."

Lacey couldn't speak if her life depended on it. She'd never experienced anything to compare to what he'd just done. He hadn't even taken off her panties. Hell, she would agree to just about anything if it meant he'd do that again.

Completely sated and wonderfully relaxed, Lacey decided to close her eyes and savor the satisfaction for just a moment, though when she did Nick's weight lifted. Curious, she opened them again. He was sitting in the couch's matching blue recliner adjacent to her, his head in his hands.

She lifted to a sitting position by sheer force of will. "Nick, what's the matter?"

He lifted his head and stared at her. "Baby, I need a shower. A damn cold one. If I don't get it quick, I'm liable to jump you."

Lacey got up from the couch, wearing only the damp thong panties, and walked over to stand directly in front of him. She stood so he was eye level with her breasts then brazenly asserted, "One good turn deserves another." While he watched, she slowly got down on her knees in front of him, placed her hands on his shoulders and gently pushed him backwards. He resisted.

"You don't have to do this. I only wanted to make you feel good. Christ, I needed to make you feel good."

Lordy, he was adorable. His expression was so loving and tender and sweet. Lacey's heart swelled. "I'm not doing this because I have to, Nick. I want to touch you, to feel your hard cock in my hands. Please don't deny me."

It was the truth. She did want to touch him. She wanted to bring him to climax in the same way he had her. She wanted to watch as he lost all control.

"God, baby, I'm so fucking hard for you right now. I'm afraid I won't be gentle, and I don't want you afraid of me."

Even his voice sounded ruthless, but she wasn't letting him go to a cold shower. "Then don't be gentle," she whispered. "Nothing you do could ever frighten me. I trust you."

She leaned forward and licked his nipple, touching the curling dark hair with her tongue. She heard him groan then he grabbed the back of her head and pulled her forward. She licked a sensual path down his muscled chest to his flat stomach.

"Do you like that?" she asked in a hushed tone. "Do you like my tongue on you, Nick?" She thought she heard him mumble something. She was sure it was as close to a yes as she was going to get.

"That's good, because I love tasting you." She leaned back and unzipped his already unbuttoned pants. They weren't loose fitting, but she was able to reach inside to cup him.

"You are so hard...so big." She couldn't keep the shock out of her voice.

"For you, baby, hard for you," he gruffly replied.

She pulled her hand free and started to yank his pants down, desperate to see him, to touch him without any barriers. Lacey had never felt so wild before. So anxious to stroke. To feel with her tongue. Make love with her mouth.

It was a major turn-on. Her own desire mounted again at the thought of giving him oral pleasure. She always assumed it was only the man that benefited. How wrong. She'd been wrong about a lot of things. She also knew in her heart that it would not be the same for her. Only with Nick could she melt this way.

"Help me take your pants off, Nick."

He raised his buttocks off the chair then pushed his pants and boxers down to his ankles. He sat back again and watched her. Tracked her every movement like a jungle cat ready to pounce.

It thrilled her to have Nick's warm brown eyes zeroed in on her. Lacey looked at his rigid length then back up at him. She smiled naughtily. "I'm one lucky girl."

She wrapped her hand around the base of him and touched his dripping tip with her tongue. She tasted his male essence and salty arousal.

His fingers dug deep into her hair, clutching her scalp. She peered up at him, and while they locked eyes, Lacey opened her mouth and sucked him deep. She watched as he threw his head back and groaned. She took him in farther then slid his hot length all the way out again. She teased the bulbous head with her tongue and heard him curse. She smiled, enjoying herself. Suddenly, his gentleness was gone and he took the lead right back.

"You're playing with fire, baby," Nick growled then grabbed handfuls of her hair on both sides of her head, and guided her down until her mouth was stuffed full with his girth. His balls pressed against her chin, and Lacey moaned in delight. She closed her eyes, bent her head slightly and sucked him down her throat.

He was buried balls deep inside of her mouth now, and she knew he was all but ready to explode. She'd won their little game of tug-o-war. Of course, she didn't think Nick was all that unhappy about losing.

She continued to suck on him, licking and teasing then deliberately pressed her naked breasts against his hair-roughened thighs, massaging her aching nipples against his skin. As she swirled her tongue around his heavy length and played with the slit at the very tip, Nick lifted his hips off the chair and pushed into her mouth so far she nearly gagged. Lacey took him even higher when she cupped his sac and squeezed. He bucked and clutched at her head, fucking her face then let out a roar and exploded. She drank every drop, hungry for his hot, salty fluid.

She raised her head and licked her lips clean. Giving him a much too naive smile, Lacey teased, "Was that to your liking, kind sir?"

"Damn, woman."

He looked at her quizzically for a moment, while he took a moment to catch his breath. Finally he mumbled, "You continue to surprise me, baby."

"Do you still need a cold shower?" she asked, feigning innocence.

He looked at her as if she'd lost her mind and let out a deep, belly laugh. "No, I definitely do not." Then he grinned and asked, "Does this mean you'll do that every time I feel the need for a cold shower?" His eyes lit up at the prospect.

It was her turn to laugh.

Chapter Seven

Damn, what a way to start the day, Nick thought with male satisfaction. He could seriously get used to this. He buttoned his jeans and stood. Just as he was about to go to the kitchen to put something together for breakfast, he heard a tiny tinkling noise. He looked around the room and realized the sound came from Lacey's purse.

Her cell phone.

She was in the bathroom, doing whatever women did after an orgasm, so he moved to answer it for her. He grabbed her purse off the table by the front door where she'd haphazardly tossed it the night before. If that bastard Evan was calling to apologize, he had another thing coming.

He located the phone in a little zipper compartment and flipped it open. "Hello."

An annoyed voice on the other end snarled, "Who the hell is this?"

The deep baritone didn't sound like Evan. That pissed him off further. Just how many men had her cell number? "Nick. Who the hell is this?"

"Nick?" the voice said, as if puzzled by that revelation.

Nick gritted his teeth. "That's what I said. Now you feel like telling me who you are or am I going to have to hang up on you?"

The guy had the nerve to chuckle before replying, "Nick, it's me, Blade."

Oops. Way to go, Nick. "Oh, sorry about that, Blade. I didn't recognize your voice."

"So I gathered." There was a pause, and then, "Uh, what are you doing answering my sister's cell at six o'clock in the morning?"

Oops again. He definitely was not winning any points with Lacey's oldest brother. Blade was a difficult man at the best of times, and he was incredibly too protective of his baby sister.

"She spent the night at my place."

Nick was a grown man, and he had absolutely nothing to hide.

Except the minor detail that he was teaching Lacey how to please a man.

"Oh?"

Just the one word, but Nick could still hear Blade's disapproval. He sighed. "Blade, your sister's been through a tough breakup, and I didn't want her to be alone last night." Well, it was partially true. Her family didn't need to know every fucking detail of their relationship. Besides, he'd already been through the third degree with Merrick. How many times must a man go through the Spanish Inquisition?

There was silence for a moment then Blade grumbled, "Yeah, I heard about Evan and Christy. I never liked that little weasel."

Nick wasn't sure which of the two Blade referred to, Evan or Christy. Blade didn't elucidate.

"I'm thinking Evan may like to know what I think about guys who treat my sister like dirt."

Oh man, Lacey would not appreciate any interference from Blade. According to Merrick, Blade had already called Evan. Anything beyond that was sure to set Lacey's independent streak off. She considered herself a grown woman, able to take care of her own affairs. But, knowing Blade, he would do as he pleased. Nick couldn't help but like the way the man's mind worked. Nick had wanted to be the one to pound Evan into the ground. And yet, if he left it to Blade, Lacey wouldn't be mad at him, she'd be mad at her brother and Evan would still get pounded. A win-win situation. Besides, Lacey would forgive her brother. She always did whenever he pulled his older brother routine. Which was often.

"The way I hear it, you already called and threatened Evan."

"It wasn't enough. Lacey deserves better. I want Evan to hurt."

Nick just shook his head. "Blade, you really are crazy."

"Yeah, I've been told that a time or two. So, you think I can talk to Lacey or what?"

It was his turn to chuckle. Blade wasn't much for small talk, that much was for certain. How could the two of them even be related? Lacey was all breezy sunshine and Blade was a great big thundercloud. Amazing.

"Sure, I'll go get her."

Nick took the phone with him and went down the hall to the bathroom. He knocked once and called out, "Lacey, your brother is on the phone."

She whipped the door open and asked, "Which one?"

"Blade."

He started to hand her the phone when she stopped him with a whispered, "You didn't tell him about us did you?"

81

That definitely wasn't what he wanted to hear. "Are you ashamed?" His words matched her low tone as he sucked in a breath, not at all sure he wanted to hear her answer.

Her eyes softened and she reached to touch his cheek with her hand. "Not on your life," she said. "But you know my family. They'll drive us nuts with questions and meddling. Well-intentioned meddling, but still... I'd like to keep this just between the two of us. For now."

He was beyond pleased that she had added *for now*. He bent down, placed a quick peck on her cheek then straightened.

"For now," he reiterated, and handed her the phone.

He heard her say hello before he left her to deal with her brother in private. He had a breakfast to fix and a woman to woo.

She loved him. What was she supposed to do now?

The thought kept racing through Lacey's mind from the moment she'd made love to him with her mouth. Like a schoolgirl, she'd retreated to the bathroom. Now, as she watched him happily walking off to do whatever, she knew there was no going back.

How in the world could she let herself fall in love with her best friend? He was only trying to help her, give her lessons on how to keep a guy from getting bored in bed, and she went and fell in love with the instructor. Not supposed to happen. The biggest reason behind all her failed relationships was that her heart hadn't been in it. Obviously, since she'd been keeping it locked up for the one special man who would knock her on her ass. How was she to know the special someone was Nick? What a mess.

Turning her attention to the phone, Lacey said, "Blade, what's going on? Is everyone okay?" Though Blade tended to keep odd hours, it was still unlike him to call her so early, and on a Sunday.

"Everyone's fine except you. I've been trying to track you down."

That meager statement was Blade's way of saying, "Why aren't you at home where you should be, safely tucked into your own bed?" But she was a grown woman, and Blade needed to get that through his thick skull.

"So you found me and I'm clearly fine," she said irritably.

"Yeah, at Nick's at six in the morning. He said you spent the night."

She rolled her eyes. "Your point being?"

Blade laughed, "Don't get all testy, sis. I was worried, that's all."

Now that did piss her off. "Worried? You know about Evan, too?" His silence filled her ear. Lacey nearly exploded. "Why is my personal life always front page news in this family? That's what I'd like to know!"

"Whoa, Mom was concerned so she called me." His voice was so tender that Lacey had a hard time being angry with him.

"Well, I'm fine. Nick's been...taking very good care of me." Wow, talk about hedging.

"So I gathered," Blade growled.

Why, oh why couldn't she have had sisters instead of brothers?

Lacey groaned in annoyance.

"Uh, look, that's not the only reason I called."

Blade must have heard her displeasure. Good thing, too, because she was a hair's breadth away from hanging up on him. She had done that more than once with Blade. He was just so infuriating at times. Lovable, but infuriating.

As his words registered, Lacey paused. He sounded unsure, and Blade Vaughn was never unsure. Curious, she asked, "Oh?"

"Candice Warner. You know her."

Lacey was still lost. "Yes, I do. What's your point?"

"She works out at your gym, isn't that right?" His voice turned harsh, when he continued. "I'm damned attracted to her and I'm not sure what the hell to do about it."

She couldn't believe what she was hearing. Blade, nervous? About a woman? "Candice works for Merrick. Or, rather, Chloe. She's her assistant." Lacey thought of Candice and frowned. "I'm not sure if you should get involved with her, Blade."

Blade sighed. "Yeah, I know. But my body doesn't agree."

"There are things you should know about Candice. She's not really a casual sex sort of woman."

"I gathered that when I went to Merrick's office the other day to pick him up for lunch. She went real quiet and blushed a lot the minute she saw me."

That was putting it mildly. If Blade only knew the half of it. "Uh, yeah, she's shy all right. Not your usual speed, I'm betting." Then something else occurred to Lacey. Maybe Blade was just the guy to get Candice to open up a little. "Then again, maybe she's exactly what you need to get you back among the living."

That put steel back into Blade's voice. "I'm plenty lively, dammit."

"Oh really?"

"Yeah, really."

"Then tell me this, when was the last time you spent more than a single night with a woman?"

She heard him curse a few times. "You know, for someone

who hates their family meddling you sure do your fair share of it, baby girl."

It was her turn to laugh. Blade only called her baby girl when she was getting to him. "You're just angry that I'm right."

"You don't know everything."

"What's there to know?" Then it dawned on her. Maybe there was more to the attraction that he wasn't telling. "Unless there's another reason you're so hesitant to get together with Candice. Is there more than mere chemistry here?"

He muttered something about little sisters who didn't know what was good for them, forcing Lacey to pry further.

"What is it, Blade? Out with it." Lacey grew more curious by the second. After all, Blade had never even acted remotely interested in a serious relationship before. Candice must have really done a number on him.

"I don't know if there's more to it than chemistry because I've not been able to get within ten feet of her."

She let her silence speak for her. Little sisters did indeed have their ways.

"She just seems...different to me. But it's pointless anyway, because she's too damn shy," Blade muttered.

Lacey was beyond shocked. She'd never in her wildest imaginings known Blade to give up on a woman. She had a sneaky feeling that all he really needed was a little push in the right direction.

"Blade, you could look at this another way."

"What other way is there? I'm going to have to see Candice and not touch her. That sucks, no matter which way you look at it."

Lacey laughed. "You're being too stubborn about this."

His voice was once again hard and unyielding. "I don't

mess with women like her, Lacey."

"Women like what?"

"You know what I mean. She's nice and sweet, and I'm, well, not."

"Are all men so obtuse?" She didn't bother to let him answer. "Do you really think Candice can't get just as dirty as the next girl?"

"Shit. I'd rather not think about it."

"I'll just bet. Because every time you do, you have to take a cold shower. Am I right?" She laughed at his groan "Yeah, well, never mind that. Just think of this. If you don't get up close and personal with her, that leaves the field open for other guys. Is that what you want?"

The startled sound he made let Lacey know the thought hadn't even occurred to him. "Fuck that," Blade growled.

"Exactly," Lacey said cheerfully. "So, get a pencil and paper and I'll give you her phone number then you can call her and ask if she wants to go out."

"You know her number?"

"Yep. As you already know, she's a client." And a good one, Lacey thought with pride. Candice was adamant about staying in shape and keeping her body healthy. She only wished all her clients were so vigilant.

"What's the number?" he muttered.

Lacey rattled it off, said a bit of this and that then hung up. Blade was on his own now. She'd done what she could. It was time she got back to Nick and his lessons.

Lacey only hoped she could keep Nick from inadvertently mashing her heart to bits.

Chapter Eight

When Lacey walked into the kitchen her intention was to continue Nick's lessons, but she came to a screeching halt when she saw him mixing something in a bowl and singing along to a rock song about long-legged women. He was naked above the waist and wore only the jeans he'd had on earlier. He was barefoot. Lacey found the sight wildly sexy.

He was making breakfast. For her. Geez, first he carried her to bed, now he was making breakfast. What would he do next?

Quietly, she moved up behind him, slid her arms around his waist and whispered, "Can I help?"

Nick dropped the spoon and mixing bowl and spun around. He opened his mouth to say something, but stopped and stared.

Lacey cocked her head to the side. "What?"

Nick bent low, took her face in his hands and pressed his warm lips against hers. Lacey forgot whatever it was she'd asked him. When he once again towered above her, he was smiling and his eyes were dark with arousal. "You make me crazy, do you know that?"

His arms went around her waist and his hands skimmed over her bottom. "Good crazy or bad crazy?" she managed to get out.

"Good crazy, baby." He dipped his head again and kissed the side of her neck, suckling at her throat and making her insane with need. His body, hard and chiseled to perfection, pressed up against her.

"Well, that's good then," Lacey sighed.

Nick grunted as he continued licking at her jumpy pulse. Lacey let her hands travel the expanse of his naked back, down to his waist and beyond until she was fairly clutching at his jean-clad buttocks. He was so firm and solid under her fingertips. She'd gotten to taste and touch just a little bit ago and she was still so impatient to see him in the flesh. No clothes in the way of her perusal this time. If this was all she was to have of him, she was determined to make the most of it.

When Nick arched into her pelvis, she felt the long length of his cock. "I want you. I want you to make love to me, Nick."

The vibration of his moan fueled her libido. He moved his mouth farther down to her neckline and kissed her oversensitive skin. Lacey wanted to make him understand just how badly she wanted him.

"I want you inside of me," she begged shamelessly. "Every hard inch of you. Please, Nick."

Nick lifted his head away and stared at her. She wondered if he could see the raw, uncontrolled desire on her face. She'd used the term "make love", not "have sex". She worried now that she'd gone too far.

"I want you, too, Lace." She lit up with eager delight, thankful he wasn't bolting. "But, for me this isn't a one shot deal, baby. I want more than just this once with you. Understood?"

Uh-oh. He was moving too fast, and Lacey so badly wanted to run. She didn't know how he felt about her. Whether he was just scratching an itch or if there was more behind his statement. She was all too aware of her own feelings, however. She'd gone this far, she may as well put another chunk of her heart on the line.

"What are you saying?" It was imperative he be clear. Lacey needed to know she wasn't reading too much into his words.

He cupped her face in his hands and held her still. "I'm saying you belong to me after this." His deep voice was rough with the heat of his emotion. "I'm through watching you with other men. It's nearly driven me insane. If you have a problem with that, say so now."

Lacey didn't know what to say. From the beginning of this odd arrangement, she'd worried she would be the one getting too emotionally involved. That she'd be the one to bear the scars of their encounter. Now she knew Nick was putting his heart on the line, too. A tremendous weight lifted away and she wanted to shout to him everything in her heart, but the look in his eyes held her back. He needed her and she needed him. Declarations of love everlasting could wait...just a little while longer.

Instead, Lacey gave him an easy answer. "I don't have a problem with that."

He'd have to settle for that, Lacey thought stubbornly. After all, there were limits as to how far a girl would go. She didn't want to end up a blithering idiot if he chose to walk away.

Nick rewarded her with a smile, his eyes turning hot and wild, as he started backing her towards the kitchen table.

"Ever have sex on a kitchen table, baby?"

"Uh, no." Lacey turned and looked at the large oval slab of oak. Skeptical, she asked, "Er, is that thing going to hold us?"

"Oh, yeah."

He picked her up and plopped her down on top of it, only releasing his hold long enough to yank her shirt up and off.

"I have to taste you, baby," he groaned. "I need to know if you're as sweet as I remember."

Lacey laughed at the absurdity of his words. "It wasn't all that long ago."

He lowered his head and mumbled something about short-term memories against her nipple then pushed her backwards until she lay flat against the cold, hard surface of the tabletop. When his mouth grazed her flesh, all reason fled. He had the most addicting way of knowing exactly how she liked to be touched. The teasing scrape of his teeth against her flesh drove her to clutch his head in both hands and pull him more firmly against her. The strokes of his tongue on her nipples turned her sex liquid. She lifted her legs, wrapped them around his waist and pulled his pelvis forward to meet hers.

Nick lifted away from Lacey's breast and stared as if in awe at the glistening wet orb. "I just love the way you're built." He cupped both breasts in his hands and squeezed, wringing a whimper out of her. "Your perfect tits are so fresh and lush." He looked into her eyes as he said, "And all mine."

Self-consciously, Lacey mumbled, "I'm not lush." She thought again of Christy's bountiful chest and wanted to cringe.

"Just my size." Nick grinned then leaned down and kissed each of her nipples lightly and bit the turgid peaks. This time when he looked back into her eyes, she saw a fire burning that hadn't been there before. Lacey wanted him to take her, hard and fast, but he seemed hesitant.

"Don't ever put yourself down again," he warned then pulled her off the table and hitched her higher around his waist. He began walking them out of the kitchen without another word.

Lacey was confused. On fire, but horribly confused. "I thought—"

"Yeah, so did I, but I've changed my mind. I want you in my bed instead."

Lacey was starting to get seriously annoyed with Nick's high-handed attitude. Deciding to take advantage of the fact that her legs were still firmly wrapped around him, Lacey squeezed, hard, gaining his attention immediately.

"What about what I want? Did you even bother to consider that?" she snapped, feeling a wild need to scream.

His smile rocked her right off her axis. "Ah, now we're getting somewhere. This is the way I want to see you. Full of fiery passion and doing something about it. You've not been very forthcoming with what you want, Lace. So, it's been up to me to decide what was best."

"What's best?" she ground out from between clenched teeth. "Are you trying to piss me off? It's not like I've been all docile and crap."

He shrugged. "I am the sex instructor, remember?"

"Yeah, but it's not as if I'm a submissive little lamb. You of all people know it."

Lacey wriggled and pushed against him until he reluctantly set her back on her feet. She put her hands on her hips and all but declared, "I won't have you deciding things for me. I am all for a guy being forceful and dominant, but pushy and arrogant is another thing altogether."

He leaned down until he was nose to nose with her. "That," he said in a seductive voice, "is lesson number three, my little spitfire."

Lacey scowled. "Lesson three?"

Nick took her hand off her hip and brought it to his mouth. He kissed each fingertip then slowly licked and bit at her sensitive skin. She could come with the smallest touch from him. It had been such a chore to gain a single orgasm from a man before Nick came along. It was humbling and stimulating at the same time.

"You aren't the kind of woman to follow along, Lacey. I only gave you a little reminder."

His eyes heated as he took in her naked, heaving breasts. In her anger, she'd forgotten she was standing topless in front of him. He hadn't.

"Your pleasure is up to you." He stroked a finger over one soft swell then down the proud and perky peak. "Tell me what you want. Tell me what feels good. Give me your fantasies, baby."

He guided her hand to his groin and seemed pleased when she curled her fingers around him.

Using his finger and thumb, Nick pinched her nipple. "Open up to me, Lace."

Lacey felt exhilarated and more turned on than ever. She'd never given a thought to taking the lead when it came to sex. It seemed natural the man would direct the show. With Evan, she didn't think she'd ever once been asked about her fantasies, about what made her insides tremble.

Lacey lifted her other hand to Nick's waist and began unbuttoning the fly of his jeans. "First, I don't want a bed," she popped the button free and leisurely slid down the zipper, "and I don't want the table, either. Later maybe, but not yet." She licked her lips in anticipation of seeing his warm, hard cock again. Of having him in the palm of her hand, literally. "I want the floor," she said in a throaty voice, "and I want to be on top."

"Damn." He growled and leaned in to kiss her, but she turned and walked over to the couch, her breasts jiggling as she walked. Without missing a beat, she pushed the coffee table to one side of the room then smiled coyly at him.

She crooked her finger and motioned him over. "Come here."

"Christ, I've created a monster," Nick teased. Lacey was wickedly pleased by the tiny hint of uncertainty she detected in his voice.

"I don't know if I'm capable of letting you be in control. But, damn I'm definitely ready to give it the old college try."

In two long strides, Nick was standing directly in front of her, apparently ready to do anything and everything she wanted. He crossed his arms over his chest and grinned at her.

Lacey didn't have a clue as to what she was doing, but decided to wing it. "Lie down, on your back," she commanded. Excitement rose a notch when he started to do as she bid. But she stopped him quickly and ordered, "After you take off your clothes."

Nick held her gaze while he slid his already unfastened jeans down his hips and legs. He tossed them to the couch, doing the same with his boxers. He lay down on the carpeted floor, crossed his arms under his head and smiled like the big jungle cat he was.

Lacey licked her lips at the sight of Nick's impressive body spread out like a sexy offering. "Now, I've got you right where I want you," she murmured.

Lacey undid her button-fly shorts, slithered them and her thong panties down the length of her legs. She stepped out of them and stood completely nude in front of Nick.

"Christ, you're so fucking hot, Lacey. You take my breath away. I'd love to see you like this every morning."

Lacey's heart swelled at Nick's romantic words. She hadn't known that aspect of him and now she was wondering how she could have missed it. Her eyes were finally open and she saw everything for the first time.

She stared at Nick's cock, turned on by the way it jutted proudly upward, hard and throbbing with vitality. As she watched, a pearly drop of come appeared on the bulbous head.

"I want you to fuck me. I want you inside of me so bad I'm actually burning from it," she breathed. "But first I want your tongue on me. I liked what you did earlier and this time I don't want anything in the way."

Lacey stepped over his torso so she stood above his face, giving him an unhindered view of her pussy. Leisurely, she lowered herself onto him until her mound just barely touched his mouth, teasing him with the scent and nearness of her. She watched as Nick inhaled and let out a rough growl then grabbed her hips in both hands and pulled her down so hard she thought she'd topple. He used his fingers to spread her swollen sex lips apart and licked at her greedily.

Lacey thrust against him, her body wild at the first contact of his tongue on her clit. She anchored herself with her hands on the floor on either side of his head and ground into his face. A ragged breath escaped him as he licked and sucked at her with mad hunger. Lacey began to buck against him, quivering and shuddering. She lost it, flung her head back and cried out Nick's name. The climax that ripped through her went on and on, the pleasure never-ending as she came into her lover's hungry mouth.

Once her body calmed, Lacey started to scoot off Nick's face, but he stopped her with his hands on her hips. He placed a soft kiss to her clitoris before letting her move down his torso.

"I need you, baby," Nick said fiercely.

She needed him just as badly. Needed him in every way a woman needed the man she loved. Overwhelmed with emotion, Lacey had to look away before she embarrassed herself. She started to move down his body eager to straddle his hips, but

Nick simply lifted her up and sat her down onto his waiting cock. His engorged length filled her completely in one smooth stroke. He was so big. Her body squeezed tight around him as if made for him.

"Oh God, Nick."

"Yeah, me, too, baby," he rasped, and he started moving.

His movements were slow at first then more urgent, until Lacey remembered she was supposed to be running the show. She clenched her inner muscles as a warning and Nick cursed from the pleasure of having his cock gripped by her silken flesh. He looked at her with curiosity, and she murmured, "Let me."

One side of his mouth crooked up. "Ride me, cowgirl."

And she did.

Lacey rotated her hips and moved up and down, fucking him the way she wanted. Raising her body up just high enough that his dick nearly came out of her then sliding slowly back down again.

She made love to him like that for what seemed like forever, enjoying the feel of him under her, inside of her, touching her everywhere at once. Her excitement began to mount once again and Nick reached between their bodies and rubbed her clit with his calloused thumb. The sweet friction sent her flying over the edge. Lacey began thrusting up and down, faster and harder. As she came a second time, she heard Nick moan her name and he was right there with her, filling her with his warm seed.

Chapter Nine

Lacey awoke several minutes later, her body heavy and sore. She lay on top of Nick. His cock was only semi-hard inside of her now. His arms were tight bands around her and his legs were entwined with hers. Lacey had never felt so comfortably surrounded. She started to move—there were things they needed to say to each other—but when she did, Nick only tightened his hold.

"Where are you going, baby?"

His eyes remained closed, his voice gravelly from sleep. She couldn't imagine anything sexier. "I need to get up. Parts of me that I never even knew existed are sore."

Lacey watched as he slowly opened his sweet brown eyes and that terribly talented mouth of his curved up into a boyish smile.

Captivated, Lacey asked, "What are you grinning at?"

Nick's arms loosened and he began massaging down her back to her buttocks. "I'm grinning because I've got an incredibly sexy woman naked and on top of me."

She smiled right back at him and whispered, "Well then," and proceeded to moan as his fingers kneaded and worked at her thigh muscles. God, the man had great hands. She gave herself a mental shake. They needed to clear the air and she couldn't let him sidetrack her. She wriggled and squirmed until he reluctantly dropped his hands away and scowled at her.

Lacey pulled herself up to a sitting position and felt his cock begin to swell inside of her. It felt deeply intimate to have him inside her body as he grew hard. She'd better get to talking, she thought, or they'd be right back at it again.

"We need to get a few things straight," she said, trying to speak around her mounting desire.

"Oh?"

He was only partly paying attention, Lacey knew, because he'd started to fondle her breasts. And, oh my, it felt good. "Where do we go from here?" she asked tentatively, "What happens now?"

Nick's eyes met hers instantly. At once, he was fully awake and alert. She loved him, but she couldn't just toss that out there. She wasn't sure he'd want her love.

"We're good together," he told her, letting his hands drift down her torso to her hips where he gripped her, keeping her from bolting like some scared rabbit.

"I think so, too, but what will that mean for our friendship?"

Nick moved her pelvis, rocking her back and forth on his cock, and muttered, "Why should it affect our friendship, baby?" He moaned, "Christ, I've never had such great sex, and I can't see a single reason why that shouldn't continue."

All at once, Lacey grew cold, her body vibrating with anger. She slipped off him and jumped to her feet. She moved out of his reach before he could even blink. Nick slowly stood. Lacey could feel his gaze on her as he tracked her frantic movements about the room to gather up her clothes.

"What the hell did I say?" Nick grumbled, shattering the moment further.

She glared daggers at him as she put her crop top back on and cursed a few times while she put on her jean shorts.

Nick walked over to her, grabbed her arms, and shook her. "Will you talk to me, damn it?" His voice rose with his temper.

Lacey couldn't breathe, she was so mad. So hurt. She'd been a fool thinking he cared about her. When would she ever learn!

"Get your hands off." Her voice was steady and deliberate, completely incongruent with her heart.

Nick's eyes turned dark. "No." His voice was a whip of command.

Lacey smiled a warning and relaxed her body. "I do know karate."

A shadow of alarm crossed his face. She waited for him to loosen his hold. When he did, she took advantage and ran to his front door. She grabbed her purse and slammed out of the house.

Once outside, the sound of Nick's angry voice calling her name drifted to her, but she ignored him. Her legs shook as she stepped off his porch and began walking down his driveway. With no way to get home and no shoes, Lacey was basically screwed. None of it mattered, not anymore. Losing her best friend and the only man she'd ever loved in one fell swoop eclipsed everything else.

Tears streamed down her cheeks and her stomach hurt so bad she thought she was going to throw up. Nothing had ever felt so horrible.

"Love sucks," she mumbled on a quivery breath. She heard a wheezy cough and turned to see Nick striding after her. His hair was all over his head, and he only had on a pair of hastily donned jeans. He was bare-chested, barefoot and gorgeous as hell. He was also frowning something fierce.

She almost smiled. Almost. She turned back around and started moving faster when he called her name.

"Lacey, wait, please."

She flipped her hair behind her shoulders and kept walking.

"I love you, Lace," Nick said on a panting gasp.

She turned around and gaped at him. He came right up to her and took her chin in his hand, frowning when he saw her tears. "Oh, baby."

He kissed her cheeks, her eyelids and her lips, before pulling away just a fraction of an inch. "Don't cry, please. You never cry. I'm so damn sorry," he said softly.

Lacey cried even harder. "You can't mean it. You said it was great sex. What about that?" she tossed back at him around sniffles.

"I would have said anything to keep you with me. You've never given me a single hint that you wanted more than sex. I thought if I told you the truth I'd lose you."

Lacey's tears turned to wild, hiccupping sobs, only now it was from the joy filling her heart and soul.

Nick, the poor, misunderstood man, ground out, "Christ, if it will make you stop crying, you can use some of that karate on me."

Lacey laughed and launched herself into Nick's arms, nearly knocking them both to the ground. She grabbed handfuls of his hair and pulled him down for a scorching kiss. When she released him, he stared at her with so much love and tenderness it made her confess her own feelings.

"I love you, too, you crazy idiot."

He grinned stupidly down at her and kissed her repeatedly.

When he finally came up for air, he looked at their

surroundings, and chuckled. "Uh, maybe we should take this back inside. We seem to be creating quite a stir."

Lacey glanced around Nick's neighborhood. An elderly woman across the street squinted in her disapproval and a teenage boy mowing the lawn seemed rather rapt by their behavior. If they didn't move off the street, the boy was liable to cut off his own foot.

Taking him by the hand, Lacey practically ran back to his house. Once she had him inside, she slammed him up against the back of the door and asked in breathless wonder, "Did you really mean what you said?"

He sobered instantly as he stroked her tangled hair away from her face with both hands. She wondered about his side, but if he was still in pain, it didn't register on his face.

"I've loved you for awhile now, Lacey. I love you more than life itself." His words were so soft she nearly missed them. "It's killed me seeing you with other men."

She couldn't believe what she was hearing. "I had no idea," she uttered in shocked surprise.

"Why do you think I came up with this stupid plan to give you lessons?" His hands traveled down her back to her ass, cupping the round globes. "You wanted to be friends, and at first so did I. It didn't take me long to figure out it wasn't enough. I wanted a life with you. It was always only you. The way I was raised, it was cold and lonely. But from the first time I met you, I felt like I'd come home. I never really understood what I was missing until you walked into my life."

Nick's hands drifted around to her front where he deftly unbuttoned her shorts. Slipping them down her legs, he cupped her soft mound in one hand. Apparently, she'd forgotten her panties as well as her shoes. She heard Nick's impatient groan.

"Tell me you want me, Lacey. And I don't mean for just

tonight. I want forever," he demanded. "Nothing less will do anymore."

Lacey's heart raced and her body was on fire. She was wildly, madly in love. "Oh, I've been so incredibly blind. I wish I'd known the way you felt, but I'm just so glad you didn't give up on me. I do want you, Nick, forever," she moaned.

She stepped out of her shorts, reached between their bodies and swiftly undid his jeans. She wrenched them down his long, powerful legs. Without waiting another second, he lifted her up and shoved her down onto his waiting cock.

"Put your legs around me, baby," he rasped, and when she did, he clutched her ass and began pumping into her warm, tight sheath. "Say it again. Tell me you love me."

"I love you, Nick. Forever." Lacey fairly screamed the words as she climaxed in his loving embrace.

Nick thrust into her hard one last time then he poured himself inside her. "I love you, too, baby. Forever."

Epilogue

"Did you have to call both your brothers?"

Lacey patted Nick's cheek and said soothingly, "Think of it this way. The sooner everything's packed, the sooner we can be alone together."

He glanced around Lacey's apartment, now almost bare, and smiled. "Yeah, I guess you're right." He frowned when he saw Blade staring at him, yet again. "Blade keeps looking at me as if he wants to do serious harm to my person."

Lacey looked over at her oldest and most unruly brother and whispered, "Aw, he's just trying to intimidate you. His bark is worse than his bite, believe me."

Nick's brow quirked up at her naïveté. "Yeah, to you maybe," he said tenderly, "but he sees me as the guy who's fucking his baby sister."

Nick still wasn't sure why he'd let Lacey talk him into calling not one, but both of her brothers in to help on moving day. It was their one-month anniversary, which was a special event and the perfect day for Lacey to move in with him since her lease was finally up.

He was thrilled he would finally be sharing his home with her. They'd no longer be going back and forth from place to place or from bed to bed, but he still felt like a bug in a jar with Lacey's brothers staring at him.

He'd spoken to Merrick earlier in the week, wanting to prepare him for the fact Lacey wasn't yet ready to marry, but she was willing to move in with him. Merrick had frowned and mumbled a lot, but he'd resigned himself to the fact Lacey was a woman with a mind of her own and no one, not even her brothers, was going to force her into marriage.

One at a time, Nick could have handled them, but both together made quite an intimidating pair. The doorbell rang, interrupting his thoughts, and Lacey moved off to answer it. Nick was left alone. As if of one mind, both brothers walked toward him. Ah, time for the much-anticipated interrogation, Nick thought as he accepted the unavoidable.

When they reached his side, Blade spoke first. "I have one question for you." When Nick indicated for him to go on, Blade asked menacingly, "You planning on marrying her?"

"Lay off, Blade," Merrick ground out—bless him—in a feeble attempt at defense. Blade stood there, silent and watchful. Both brothers looked so much alike it was eerie. They could have been twins, except for an inch or two in height and Merrick's clean-shaven face, as Blade had a full mustache.

Nick rolled his eyes at Blade's absurd question. "Of course, what the hell did you think I was going to do with her?"

Blade never got the chance to answer, as they became aware of Lacey's raised voice. They turned toward her to see what had her in an uproar. Evan, the dickhead, was back. Nick's face turned red with rage when Evan grabbed hold of Lacey. Blade started toward the two of them, no doubt ready kill Evan, but Nick stopped him with a hand on his forearm.

"Just wait a minute, Blade."

Blade's voice was low and deadly when he asked, "You're going to stand here while that asshole puts his hands on my sister?"

"Trust me. She's not a helpless little girl anymore," Nick answered. He cringed as he saw the look on Lacey's face. "Oh, shit, he's in for it now. She's smiling."

"What the hell is that supposed to mean?" Blade snarled then turned to look at Lacey.

Both of the Vaughn men stood in silent shock as they watched Lacey's leg come up and connect with Evan's jaw, knocking him flat on his ass.

"Holy shit!" they exclaimed in shocked unison.

"Damn right." Nick beamed, ridiculously proud and turned on at the same time. "That's my girl."

Blade and Merrick began talking at once, but Nick couldn't take his eyes off Lacey. She was so damned beautiful standing there with her hair in a cute ponytail and her pert little ass encased in a pair of soft, tight, cotton shorts. He started walking toward her, but it was Blade's turn to stop him.

"What?" Nick said absently, still keeping an eye on the extremely disgruntled Evan.

"Where do you think you're going? I wasn't through with you."

"I'm going to make sure Evan doesn't make the mistake of getting up." Then he turned to Blade, looked him square in the eyes and flatly stated, "I love your sister, Blade, and I swear I would never do anything to hurt her. That's all that should matter to you."

Blade seemed to consider his words then nodded, apparently pleased with his answer because he actually smiled. Merrick smiled as well. Soon, both of them smacked him on the back in a show of approval. Nick made his escape before they broke a bone or injured a vital organ with their friendly taps.

He came right up to Evan, pulled him to his feet and

punched him. Blood spurted out of his nose as he clutched and groaned. The two Vaughn brothers in the background cheered him on. "Get lost, dickhead," Nick growled to Evan.

With immense male satisfaction, he watched as Evan scrambled and stumbled his way down the walk.

Nick slammed the door shut, grabbed a startled Lacey in his arms and kissed her full on the mouth. He parted her lips with his tongue and breathed between her lips, "I love you, baby, forever."

Lacey sighed and sank into his kiss, repeating the words back to him with all her heart and soul.

A sense of completeness settled over him. No doubt, their relationship had only just begun, but he was confident that watching the girl of his dreams drift away from him was a thing of the past.

He had a future of mystery and excitement to look forward to with his best friend and lover by his side every step of the way. It didn't get any better than that.

Keeping her in his arms, Nick leaned back enough to see the drowsy look on Lacey's face. He pushed a few strands of her soft, dark hair behind her ears and asked, "So, what did he want anyway?"

Lacey rolled her eyes. "Can you believe he wanted me back?"

Nick had figured as much. "What happened to Christy?"

She tried valiantly to contain a laugh. "He caught her on his dining room table with a man she picked up while jogging in the park."

Nick smirked. "Serves the bastard right."

"That's what I told him."

They both started laughing. As they imagined Evan walking

in on such a display, they laughed harder.

"I also told him he might want to go see a doctor and get tested for HIV since it's clear Christy isn't all that finicky about who she sleeps with. He went a little white after that. The idiot."

Nick let his finger trail a path down her cheek to her neck. He stroked her pulse and felt it quicken under his fingertip.

"So, what made you want to kick him?" he asked, only half interested in the conversation, because Lacey had begun to smooth her hands down his sides.

Lacey licked her lips, her gaze never once straying away from his mouth. She was just as aroused as he. Damn, if only they were alone.

"Lacey?" Nick prompted.

"Hmm?" she murmured, dazed.

"Why'd you kick Evan?"

Lacey blinked, looked into his eyes and said "Oh, right. Well, he told me I was the best thing that ever happened to him."

"And that made you want to kick him? Seriously?"

"No. To tell you the truth, I just felt like it."

"You are one scary lady."

"You don't sound upset by that."

He winked and leaned down to whisper into her ear, "Seeing you in action is a major turn on for me, baby."

Lacey groaned. "Lord, I wish we were alone."

"My thought exactly," he growled. Unable to help himself any longer, Nick let his tongue dart out and touch the soft shell of her ear. He tasted the sweetness of her silky skin and instantly went hard. He heard a few grumbles from the other side of the room and realized Lacey's brothers were getting quite an eyeful.

Nick lifted a few inches, stared hard at Lacey and promised, "Tonight, after you're completely moved in and your family has finally left us alone, you and I are going to have our own private little party."

Lacey beamed up at him and asked, "Because of our one month anniversary?"

Nick shook his head. "Nope."

Lacey gave him a puzzled look. "Er then why?"

"Because I finally got the woman of my dreams," Nick answered tenderly as he imagined waking up to a soft, warm Lacey every day for the rest of his life.

Nope, it definitely didn't get any better than that.

Tasting Candy

Dedication

To Kelley Nyrae. We started this journey together and it has been so much fun bouncing ideas around with you! Your self-discipline and drive inspires me greatly.

To my lovely reader, Heather. Your excitement over my stories keeps me tapping at the keys. Thanks for all the moments you dropped everything to give me a second set of eyes. I'm very glad you found your way over to *After Dark* and became a part of our crazy family.

Chapter One

He was a glutton for punishment. Blade had no other explanation for coming to Tough Bodies Gym. His mother had put him up to it. She always worked things out to her advantage. He was a thirty-four year old man and yet he'd never been able to say no to Mom.

His gaze swept the impressive gym, and he felt a surge of pride. Blade's construction business, Vaughn Building and Remodeling, had been contracted to build it and they'd done a fine job.

But as he watched his sister Lacey show Candice Warner the proper way to do a crunch, Blade groaned. Up, down, then it started all over again. Blade's blood heated and his cock turned hard just watching Candice's firm, perky body shift in sinuous, slow movements. Her face contorted as she worked through the burn, her body dripping from the exertion. He could easily picture her in the throes of one hellacious orgasm.

She wore a pair of black workout shorts and one of those bra-like exercise shirts. Christ, she was put together just right, too. What the hell was she working out for anyway? From his vantage point, she didn't need to improve her figure. She was perfect the way she was. Blade swiped a hand over his face and practically moaned at his own weakness, which, of course, was Candice.

It had been that way from the first. He'd walked into his brother's office all wound up from work, then he'd spotted her. She'd glanced up at him from her desk with those innocent blue eyes, her sandy-brown hair pulled into a messy bun, and he'd immediately forgotten his own name. She'd smiled sweetly at him, and he'd gotten hard as a railroad spike.

Blade had shamelessly given her the once over, noticing the enticing blush that had heated her ivory cheeks. She'd turned all pink and warm right before his eyes, making Blade ache to take her against the office door and fuck her right there on the spot, make her scream out his name and beg him for more. From that moment, he'd been hooked.

Magnetism, karma, chemistry, whatever the hell it was, he knew he would have to have her or die.

But damn if he wasn't too chicken shit to make the first move. He'd always been the aggressor with women, but for some inexplicable reason, Candice made him hesitate. In some deep part of his soul, Blade knew that he shouldn't be screwing around with someone so innocent. He was the wolf to her Little Red Riding Hood.

Still, when he'd confided all this to Lacey, she'd laughed and told him that if he didn't make a move on Candice then some other man would. The thought still pissed him off.

Shoring up his nerve even while he reminded himself that this was nothing more than an errand for his mother, Blade moved farther into the spacious, private workout room and cleared his throat. The action had the desired effect. Lacey glanced his way, while Candice bounded to her feet. She was always such a jumpy little thing.

"Blade, what are you doing here?" Lacey asked as she rose to greet him with a hug. Candice's gaze darted around the room as if searching for an escape route. She seemed intent on getting away from him.

"Mom wanted me to drop this off. And to make sure you're coming to the cookout tonight." Blade pulled the business card out of his front shirt pocket and dropped it into Lacey's hand.

"Crystal's Weddings and Banquets, Inc." Lacey rolled her eyes. "Oh, for crying out loud, Blade."

He threw up his hands in self-defense. "Hey, don't shoot the messenger."

Deep down, Blade was pleased as punch that their mother was pushing Lacey on the whole matrimony issue. Lacey had fallen in love with Nick Stone, a man she'd been best buds with for years. While he respected Nick as a man, all that had changed the minute he became intimately involved with his baby sister. Blade wasn't at all happy that she and Nick were living together. He was just old-fashioned enough to want to see a ring on Lacey's finger. It'd go a long way toward giving him peace of mind, as well as ensuring Lacey's future.

Lacey wadded up the small card and threw it toward the corner. It landed in the wastebasket. "I've told her when Nick and I decide to get married, she'll be the first to know." Then as an aside, she complained, "And of course Nick and I are coming to the cookout."

Blade shrugged. "Yeah, well, I think she wants to see it in writing or something."

Lacey swung around. "Where's Candice?"

"She went out the door." He ought to know; he'd been surreptitiously watching her every move.

Lacey gasped, as if startled that Candice had left the privacy of the workout room. Blade was baffled as to why that was such point of concern. Lacey moved quickly toward the entrance. Curious, Blade followed close behind.

"But why would she go out to the main floor? She never goes out to the main floor," Lacey said in a rush.

Lacey's worry for Candice became infectious. "I assumed she was going to the bathroom or something. You know, giving us a minute."

"You don't understand, she never goes out to the main floor, Blade. Never!"

"Okay, you're starting to worry me here, sis," he rumbled. "What's the big deal?"

"Just help me find her."

He could do that, Blade thought, slightly panicked now. Several minutes later, they'd still had no luck finding her. But it was Saturday, and sweaty bodies packed the room. Candice was just one woman. Such a large crowd would swallow her up.

Finally, Blade spotted her plastered against a wall. Three heavily-built weightlifters hovered over her, flirting, which pissed him off. As he drew closer, Candice appeared frozen in fear. Christ, she was scared to death.

"What the hell?" he snarled, more than ready to kick some ass.

In a few long strides, he yanked two of the huge men away from Candice. He slammed them both against the opposite wall, then glared at the third man, promising bodily harm if he so much as blinked. "You three hassling the lady?"

They all stammered at once. Blade was about to hit one of them when Lacey arrived. "Let them go, Blade," she pleaded, but he wasn't in the mood to be accommodating. "It's okay. I don't think they meant any harm."

Blade wasn't so sure. Keeping his eyes on the three idiots, he asked, "Candy, are you okay?"

"I-I'm fine." Candice's reply was so small he barely heard

her. He released the two Casanovas and watched as all three men hurried off. When he turned around, Candice was red as a beet and breathing erratically. Even more puzzling, his sister was helping her back toward the private workout room.

"Lacey?" he asked, feeling like an intruder. Lacey's stern expression forced him to hold all his questions for later. A sense of helplessness settled in his stomach as he followed behind the two women, blocking curious patrons. He might not know Candice well, but he realized she was probably embarrassed. Candice was shy and she wouldn't appreciate the gawking stares.

Once they were back in Lacey's private workout area, Blade closed the door, effectively shutting out prying eyes. Lacey seated Candice against the wall on the floor, then ran to fetch a bottle of water.

Blade stood back, watchful and unsure what to do to make the shell-shocked expression on Candice's delicate, oval face go away. She breathed easier, but now her cheeks were deathly pale. Her huge, dark blue eyes appeared to stare at nothing. She kept clenching and unclenching her fists. He was afraid she'd hurt herself if she continued to dig her fingernails into her palms.

What could the three men have done to make her panic? It didn't appear as if they'd done anything more than talk to her. Hell, there hadn't been time for more than that, but why would she get so upset over a little harmless flirting? Answers. Blade needed answers and he wouldn't get them by playing guard duty.

He closed the distance between them. Candice blinked and stared up at him, then smiled. God, she was pretty when she did that. There was such a sweet innocence about her. Every time Blade was in her presence, he felt out of her league.

He crouched in front of her and took her fists in his hands, then gently uncurled her fingers and smoothed his thumbs over the little crescent moons she'd created with her nails. "If those assholes hurt you, I'll kill them. Just say the word, Candy."

She blinked as if dazed. "No, but thank you, Blade. They didn't do anything wrong. I just had a panic attack, that's all. And my name is Candice, not Candy." His sister returned and handed Candice the glass of water, then fussed over her, breaking the fragile connection between them.

"Why did you go out to the main floor?" Lacey asked as she started to fan her with her hands. "You know how busy it gets on weekends, hun."

Candice shrugged. "I wasn't thinking. I only wanted to give you two some privacy and I thought if I could just get to the bathroom and back I'd be okay, but..." Her words trailed off and she peeked at him again, making it clear that she wasn't about to discuss the strange episode in front of him. He wanted her to open up to him, but every time the opportunity arose, she managed to wiggle away again.

Lacey massaged her arm in a soothing gesture, and a pang of envy shot through him. He wanted to be the one massaging Candice's smooth, ivory skin.

"I think we better quit for today, don't you?" Lacey said, "You should get home and take a nice warm bath. Try to relax and forget about all this."

Candice nodded and started to rise, and just that quick, Blade was there, grabbing the opportunity to touch her again. He helped her to her feet, but she stepped back as soon as she was upright. He was forced to release her or look like an idiot.

"I'm fine now, really. I'm sorry you had to take your time searching for me, Blade. I know you're a busy man." When he started to tell her he hadn't been put out, she talked right over him in that soft way she had. "I can't tell you how much it means to me that you were there to help me with those guys. Thank you."

She smiled one last smile and walked away. She retrieved her gym bag and left out a back entrance, leaving Blade to stare and wonder what the hell had just happened.

&

"The award for the biggest fool who walked the earth goes to Candice Warner," she complained. Would she ever stop thinking every man was like Lance? It didn't seem to matter that she grew physically stronger with each workout, or how well she did in her self-defense classes, she still cowered around men. She was furious with herself and also saddened now that Blade had witnessed her mental breakdown. She didn't want him seeing her as a helpless ninny.

Candice had started working at Merrick Vaughn's company, Vaughn Business Solutions, less than a year ago, and she'd loved every minute of it. Her supervisor, Chloe Vaughn, Merrick's wife, was about the best boss anyone could ask for. That was how she'd encountered Blade the first time. Candice would never forget that day as long as she lived.

He'd come to meet Merrick for lunch, and she'd nearly swallowed her tongue. He was so ruggedly handsome, so powerfully built. Dressed completely opposite to Merrick, Blade sported a pair of tight, work-worn jeans that molded to his tall, powerful frame as if made for his body alone. His white t-shirt had been dusty from work and his big, heavy, black boots had left clods of dirt on the carpet in his wake. He'd smiled at her briefly, and she'd wanted to melt into a puddle. Then he'd glanced down, noticing for the first time the mess he had made, and he'd grimaced. Even his grimace was sexy.

Candice had gone speechless when he'd bent to scoop the clods with his hands, and she'd stared unabashed at his firm backside, wishing for all the world that she was bold enough to reach out and grab a handful of him.

Destroying her composure further, Blade had walked around her desk, coming within an inch of touching her, and tossed the dirt into her trashcan. As he straightened, Blade grinned and whispered a husky apology, his dark, sinful voice turning her bones to liquid in a heartbeat.

Never in a million years would Blade ever know how close Candice had come to taking those precious clods of dirt out of the trash and spiriting them home with her as if they were sparkling diamonds.

The way he'd stared at her, all of her, as if he could see right into her private thoughts. As if he knew exactly the way he affected her and was pleased by it. It had unnerved her, and she'd tried to avoid him ever since.

"He must really think I'm nuts," Candice muttered to herself as she filled the tub with suds and hot water. The one man she'd actually been attracted to, the only man she'd thought of in a romantic way since the ordeal with Lance Markum a little over a year ago, had just witnessed her in a full-fledged panic attack. And all because a few men had flirted with her. It was beyond belief!

She slipped off her clothes, then sat in the inviting warmth, determined to regain her equilibrium. She closed her eyes and allowed the solitude to surround her and take her mind away from the sadness of the past and into her dream world, where everything was warm and men treated women with respect. She used the words her therapist, Dr. Jackie Lewis, had given her, to force her mind to focus on what could be, and not what had been.

"I have the courage to embrace my strengths. To get excited about life and to give and receive love. I have the courage to face and transform my fears." She repeated the mantra three more times before she fell asleep. The lavender soap and warm water took her off to a safe place where she could explore her desires without getting hurt.

The soft glow of a candle suffused the room. Candice wore a long, pale pink satin nightgown, and her lover stood in a pair of black silk boxers. They stared at each other for a long moment, then he smiled and beckoned her to come to him. She went willingly. When she stood a few inches from him, she smiled and allowed him to slip the straps of her gown down her shoulders and arms until the pink confection pooled at her feet.

She reached out and grasped at the edges of his boxers and slid them off his lean hips. Desire darkened his eyes as she tugged him forward. When the wet heat of his mouth closed over her nipple, suckling and tugging, Candice squirmed and clutched, edgy for more. For all of him.

Suddenly, a ring disrupted her dream, and Candice reached out, only to grasp at thin air. Her fantasy lover disappeared as she lay in a cooling tub of water and wilted bubbles. Then someone banged a fist against her door and she groaned. She couldn't even have a flaming wet dream!

"Just when things were starting to get good, too." Disgruntled, she stepped out of the tub and hurriedly dried off, but the pounding came again.

"Just a minute already," she yelled. Then fear started to creep in. Who could be knocking on her door at...well, it was really only mid-afternoon. Still, she didn't have a bunch of friends, and most anyone she knew would call first.

Candice threw on her robe, grabbed the mace she kept by

the front door and called out, "Who is it?"

"It's me, Blade."

"Blade?" she repeated with surprise and more than a touch of elation.

"Yeah, Blade Vaughn, Lacey's brother."

Candice rolled her eyes. As if she could possibly know more than one Blade. As if she wouldn't recognize the sexy, deep baritone of his voice. Candice unhooked the chain and undid the three locks, then slowly opened the door.

"What on earth are you doing here?" She thought of something else. "And how did you even know where I live?"

Blade's eyebrows shot up and his face lit with amusement. "We need to talk, and Lacey told me." With a hint of a smile playing at his lips, he asked, "Do you always answer your door wearing a robe and wielding a can of mace?"

Candice's face heated as she tucked the mace into her pocket. She'd forgotten about both her robe and the mace with Blade Vaughn standing on her doorstep. He must have come straight from the gym, because he was wearing the same clothes. With his requisite work jeans, a battered navy blue t-shirt that had seen better days and work boots, he was, as usual, devastatingly handsome. And that's when it hit her like a Mack truck. Oh god, how on earth could she have missed it?

It was him! The man in her dreams. The sinfully sexy guy she'd been making love to for the past several months. He was none other than Blade Vaughn! Candice's entire body warmed at the idea of having a flesh-and-blood reproduction of the person who'd brought her to climax, not once, but dozens of times in her dream world.

She looked at his face more closely, committing details to memory, comparing and searching. Of course, Candice thought with a heady sigh, she should have recognized him. The mustache, the deep-set eyes and broad face. Oh lord, she wondered if the rest of his body matched her dream version.

Wow.

Chapter Two

Christ, she was adorable. He would never get used to his reaction to this woman. She stood with her shoulder-length light brown hair piled atop her head, a look of total mortification on her freshly scrubbed face. She didn't even look sexily mussed—just mussed. That he could get a boner over her even when she wore an ugly brown terrycloth robe was saying something.

She always turned him on. He was going to do something about it, too. Eventually. Right now, he wanted some answers. Lucky for him, he was very good at getting them. He would coerce and railroad until he was satisfied. It was the way he operated. Candice would just have to get used to it.

"So, you going to let me in, or use that can on me?" He shrugged. One way or the other, Blade would gain entrance. "It's your choice."

Candice yanked her robe together tighter, which was a crying shame since it had started to drift open and he had been this close to a sneak peek. "Of course, please, come in." Then she moved out of the doorway and allowed him inside. He smiled, triumphant. It was a small concession, but she was so closed-up around him, entering her private domain felt like a big fucking deal.

Her living room was...dainty. Figured. Damn near

everything about Candice was dainty. It enhanced the fact he felt like a bull around her. It was cozy, though, something in the way she'd decorated. He'd expected pinks and peaches and fluffy ruffles, but it was all earth-tones, woodsy and serene. Actually, there was something sort of peaceful about her home. He wondered if she did that on purpose because of the panic attacks. Speaking of which...

"I want to know why you went ballistic today at the gym." Oh yeah, subtlety was his middle name. Jesus.

Her eyes widened. "Ballistic?" Candice asked. Suddenly, a smile slipped across her face, then a laugh bubbled up. Soon, she was practically crying from laughing so hard.

"Hell, it wasn't that funny," Blade grumbled, feeling disgruntled and not sure why. But he did like to see her smiling instead of near tears. Much better, to his way of thinking.

Candice calmed enough to say, "You just aren't the sweet-talker your brother is, are you?"

Now what the hell was that supposed to mean? "Has Merrick hit on you?" he asked, unaccountably possessive and jealous.

Blade would kill him. It didn't matter that Merrick was married to Candice's boss, Chloe, and madly, deeply in love. He'd still kill him.

"No, not at all. It's just that he's got a real way with words. He can sell anyone darn near anything with barely more than a smile. You, on the other hand, you're just the opposite. You bully and push until you get your way." She tilted her head to the side as if studying him. "Amazing that you're related."

"We are talking about Merrick, right?"

"Of course, unless you have another brother that I don't know about." She smiled as she moved away from him. He noticed she did that a lot, kept a physical distance.

"Nope, just Merrick." And to set his mind straight he asked, "Has Merrick ever flirted with you?"

"No. He's totally devoted to Chloe. I don't think he even knows other women exist."

Satisfied with that answer, he pointed to the couch. "Mind if I sit?"

She blushed, which, as he'd already discovered, turned him on. Every fucking thing she did turned him on. "Of course, have a seat." Looking down at her robe, she frowned. "I'll, uh, just go get dressed."

"I don't see why," Blade growled. His gaze traveled over her once more. Christ, his lust grew by leaps and bounds whenever he was within a mile of the woman.

"Yes, well, I'll be right back," she stammered, then flitted from the room, leaving him to his own devices.

He went over to the couch, which was the size of a love seat to him, and sat. It was forest-green with beige stripes and surprisingly comfortable. As he waited, he studied the living room and noted something strange. While the room seemed plenty lived-in and had a real homey feel, it was devoid of anything personal. Then he spotted a single photograph nestled between a bunch of paperbacks on a bookshelf in the corner. His curiosity got the better of him. Blade left the couch and went to it, drawn by the wild need to know more about the woman who had been haunting both his days and nights.

It was a snapshot of a couple standing with their arms around a tiny dark-haired girl in pigtails. The woman was obviously Candice's mother—she looked exactly like her—and the man had a bright smile on his face, as if he couldn't possibly be happier. The picture was old, though. Candice couldn't have been more than eight or nine at the time. Where were her parents now? And why just the one picture?

He left it and went back to sit on the couch, shocked at the protective instincts that kicked in at the thought of Candice being all alone in the world. He'd always had his parents, his brother and sister. They were his whole life. He couldn't imagine not having them. And he was already anticipating Merrick and Chloe having kids someday. It'd be fun to have a few curtain-climbers in the family to liven things up a bit. He'd enjoy being an uncle.

Yep, no doubt about it, without his unruly siblings, life would be as dull as a brick. Did Candice have any friends other than Lacey? Then there was the house. Blade was surprised she could afford it. No doubt, Candice made good money working at Vaughn Business Solutions, but the house was bigger than what he would have thought she could handle alone.

It was a one-storey ranch with a two-car garage and, judging by the size, three bedrooms. More than what a woman living alone needed. Being a construction contractor, Blade didn't need to see the interior to know the approximate dimensions of the rooms. Besides, a woman living by herself generally preferred an apartment. Hell, he lived in an apartment. Nevertheless, having other people around tended to make a woman feel safe. No landscaping upkeep, either. So why choose to live alone in a house that was too big for a slip of a woman like Candice?

She was certainly a puzzle. It was a good thing he loved puzzles.

When she returned, Blade's body reacted. She affected him in a way no other women ever had—and he'd definitely had his share. Women who were sexier and no doubt more eager to be in his presence. But here he was, getting all hot and bothered over a woman who wanted nothing to do with him. Which, needless to say, made him want her even more. It was crazy, but Blade couldn't deny the temptation to get to know her on an intimate level. He'd tried that already, and he'd gotten nowhere.

It was high time he did something about his secret lust. Enough of wondering how her skin would feel against his, what her lips would taste like, how she would sound during a climax. How fucking good she would feel wrapped around his cock. It kept him up at night, and running a construction company on little to no sleep was not a good idea. Hell, if he didn't get the imp out of his system, he'd end up killing himself. The way he saw it, having sex with Candice Warner was a matter of life and death.

Once he got her to bed and had his fill of her warm, welcoming body, he would be able to get back to normal and feel in control again.

Candice was completely aware of Blade Vaughn's presence in her home. Having any man inside her sanctuary was uncomfortable enough, but more so with a man as virile and masculine as Blade. He fairly exuded male confidence and sexual prowess. He was dark and savage, and she wasn't comfortable with any of it.

He sat on her couch with his large muscular legs spread wide and one elbow on the armrest, the other hand resting on his thigh. Dear lord, he had sexy forearms. She'd always liked a man's forearms, and Blade's were first-rate, strong and thick and tan from working construction. Candice gave herself a mental smack as she remembered the last man who'd caught her interest. She refused to go down that road. She would not think of the last time she'd been alone in a room with a man. Going there could only lead to disaster.

Besides, Blade was nothing like Lance. Blade didn't need to force women to have sex with him. Ha! She was pretty sure women fell at his feet, willing and ready to please. But she wasn't going down that road either. Not now, and maybe not ever again. The sooner she got the big lug out of her home, the quicker she could get back to feeling safe.

Candice had to admit that being around Blade didn't panic her. It only made her more aware of him as a man. And now she knew her crush had gone to her head and caused her to have some pretty wicked dreams. It was downright amazing the way the mind worked.

She decided the best approach would be to keep things polite and friendly. "Would you care for something to drink?" There, that sounded normal and in control.

Blade took in her appearance. She'd put on a sundress, but it was long, sleeveless and unshapely. The shape of her body was hidden beneath the pale-yellow cotton. The way his eyes heated, she might as well be standing before him in a satin teddy. He smiled at her, slung an arm over the back of the couch and asked, "Got a cold beer?"

Candice had to stop from visibly cringing. "I don't drink. Sorry." Never again, she thought with trepidation. "Just soft drinks and lemonade, I'm afraid."

"Nothing for me, thanks." His head cocked to the side as his lips kicked into a crooked grin. Suddenly, Candice couldn't think of anything but the fascinating way Blade's features softened when he did that.

"I'd much rather you sit down," he coaxed. When Candice only stared at him, his brows shot up. "I won't bite." She was sure he was going to add something to that statement, but he must have changed his mind because he went silent instead. Silent and watchful.

She moved forward and sat in the chair opposite him. No way was she going to sit next to him on the couch. That would be entirely too close for her peace of mind. She might have a panic attack. One embarrassing moment a day was her limit. Unfortunately, as soon as she was seated, he went right back to his earlier question.

"So, Lacey—being the good friend that she is—wouldn't tell me why you...panicked at the gym," he stated gruffly. "But I'm a nosy bastard and I won't let this rest until I know why you freaked when those men flirted with you." He leaned forward, and Candice could almost feel the heat in his eyes. The way he stared had her body rioting out of control. "So, out with it, Candy, because you said yourself that I don't tend to give up until I get what I want."

What she was about to tell him would probably have him running as fast as his feet would take him. The few men she'd opened up to about her date-rape had acted as if she'd somehow done something unforgivable. She hated for Blade, of all people, to feel that way, too.

"I have panic attacks whenever I'm around men." She looked down at her lap and said, "For about a year now, ever since I was raped." There, she'd said it. He would leave, and she could cry in silence.

"You were raped?"

Blade's voice sounded harsh and cold, as if the idea left a bad taste in his mouth. Feeling defensive, Candice went stiff and her voice dripped with icy venom. "Yes. And even though I've been to counseling, I still have a problem whenever I feel threatened or cornered by a man."

Blade shot to his feet and spewed out a variety of curses, some she'd never heard before. His large, strong hands balled into fists of fury at his sides and his muscles bunched beneath his t-shirt as he paced away from her. Candice wasn't sure what to do. She sat as fear crept in, helpless to stop it.

"Blade?" she managed before her throat closed. He turned

at the sound of her quivery voice. All at once, his anger seemed to melt away, and he knelt at her feet.

"Don't do that, sweetheart. I would never hurt you. Never, I swear it. I've never had a woman fear me before. Please," he begged softly, "I don't think I could stand it if I thought you were afraid of me."

She took a deep breath and let it out very slowly, calming her jittery stomach, then counted to ten. Finally able to speak, she asked, "Why did you get so angry?"

She'd begun to clutch at the skirt of her dress, and when she released the soft material, he held her hands gently in his own. "The thought of someone hurting you that way..." Blade closed his eyes tightly for a moment, then opened them, staring at her with unreleased fury lighting their icy-blue depths. "It makes me want to kill the filthy bastard."

She didn't quite know what to make of that. She'd never had a man feel anger on her behalf before. It was a new experience. And not all that unpleasant, either. "He's in prison," she said, as if that made it all okay. It didn't, of course, but knowing that Lance couldn't hurt anyone else helped ease the pain.

"I'm sorry. I know it's lame, but it's all I've got."

Blade spoke with such tenderness. It stunned her that someone with such a hard exterior could have so much compassion. She had a feeling there was a lot about Blade that would surprise her. For the first time in a long while, Candice didn't feel a terrible cloud hanging over her.

"It's not your fault." She tried a smile and observed their entwined fingers, wondering why she wasn't pulling away, wondering why her fingers pressed against his seemed so right. "I'm learning to deal with it. I just..." She shrugged and tried to explain. "I can't be around men. I get very nervous, and it just

Anne Rainey

snowballs from there."

Very gently, as if afraid of spooking her, Blade said, "So, that's what happened at the gym today?" She nodded. "I see. Do you want to talk about it? I'm a pretty good listener." She bit her lip, skeptical, and he added, "Come and sit beside me on the couch."

Her eyes must have conveyed her fear over the idea of being so close, because he quickly added, "I promise we'll just talk. It'll be okay."

He stood and tugged at her hand. Candice let him pull her to her feet, then she sat next to him. He put his arm around her shoulders and she almost shot off the couch. But his fingers began to massage, and she relaxed.

"Okay?" Blade whispered.

She nodded. It was strange to be this close to a man and not feel threatened. Dr. Jackie had been trying to get her to date again, but she hadn't felt ready. Jackie had also insisted she learn to trust again. Candice had told her she could never trust another man, no matter who that man might be. Still, sitting there with Blade...well, she had to admit it wasn't totally unpleasant.

"Do you want to tell me about it, sweetheart?"

Blade's voice was whispery soft against her cheek, and she nestled into the crook of his arm so she couldn't see his face. That helped her to open up.

"His name is Lance Markum. We worked together—before I came to work for your brother—and I'd had a mild crush on him. A bunch of the girls thought he was really something, but he'd asked me out and I felt special. I'd...I'd never been with a man before." Thinking of it all over again, Candice knew she'd been naïve.

"I was so thrilled he'd chosen me. We went to a movie, then

130

he brought me back to his apartment. He gave me something to drink. It wasn't until the next day, at the hospital, that I found out he'd drugged me." She shrugged. "I guess I was pretty naïve about the whole thing. He told me afterwards that he'd picked me because I'd be an easy mark and he'd enjoy popping my cherry."

Blade's body stiffened, so she finished. "Fortunately, that's what kept going through my mind during the trial. He was so sure I wouldn't prosecute, and I just kept thinking there wasn't a chance in hell he was ever going to get another woman alone like that." She smiled when she thought back on Lance's reaction. "The shock and panic on his face when I sat on the witness stand and told everyone what he'd done was worth every second of the humiliating cross-examination."

"Christ, I'm sorry you had to go through that." They were both silent a moment, then Blade prompted, "You had your family with you, though?"

She shook her head as her eyes filled with tears. "I was adopted by two very loving people, but they died five years ago in a plane crash, which left me with this house. It was one of those commuter flights and they were going on a second honeymoon."

Blade didn't know what to say. This small bundle of nerves had endured so much. He could easily take Lance Markum apart with his bare hands. He wanted to get him in a room alone and make him feel as helpless, as vulnerable, as he'd made Candice feel. That she'd had to deal with it all on her own made his heart ache for her. That Markum had stolen her virginity in such a vulgar way made him so mad a red haze of hate filled his vision.

Blade could never imagine what it must have been like

having to face the slimy bastard in court. But he was so proud of Candice. Her strength boggled him.

"I'm sorry about your parents, sweetheart. And I'm sorry as hell for what that bastard took from you."

Candice's shoulders slumped, then began to quiver. She was crying. It made him feel helpless and weak when a woman cried, but Lacey had told him once that sometimes a woman just needed to shed a few tears if she ever wanted to feel good again.

So Blade held Candice close while she poured out her grief, and he waited. Once she was done, he was going to set a few things straight, as there was no way he was going to let her shut him out the way she'd done with the rest of the world. She had too much to give.

Chapter Three

"I want you to come with me tonight," Blade stated.

Candice had no idea what he was talking about, but she was terribly embarrassed over her breakdown. How mortifying that twice in one day the handsome hulk had seen her in hysterics.

"Come with you?" She swiped at her swollen eyes. Trying to regain her dignity, Candice started to stand.

"Wait," Blade said, holding her firmly against him. "Just hear me out before you erect your little shield."

That got her back up. "I do not have a shield, Blade Vaughn," Candice said. "And let go of me." She was surprised when he did release her. She had to admit a twinge of disappointment that he'd ceded to her request so easily, but she was very glad he wouldn't force her. She stood, facing him and glaring. Unfortunately, he was so incredibly tall that her standing had only put her at eye level with him, which wasn't good for her equilibrium. As Blade's lips kicked up at the corners, she melted into a puddle of desire and lust. He was just too good-looking for her peace of mind.

"You definitely have a shield," he teased. "And it goes up anytime anyone gets too close."

She crossed her arms under her breasts. "If you're trying to ask me out, then you aren't doing a very good job of it."

"I'm asking you to come with me to a family cookout."

Sheer terror replaced her ire. "I'm not sure that's a good idea."

"You know half the people already, Candy, so don't go getting all jumpy on me."

It had been a long time since she'd done anything sociable, and she wasn't confident how she would react. It would be awful if she panicked in front of friends and coworkers.

Blade pried her arms apart and took one of her hands in his own. He stared at their fingers as he rattled off who would be there.

"My mom is cooking, and I know you like my mom." His deep, tender voice transfixed her. Obviously Blade took her silence as a sign that he could continue pleading his case. "Merrick and Chloe will be there, no doubt making goo-goo eyes at each other. Nick and Lacey, as well, driving Mom crazy with their 'we aren't in a rush to marry' bullshit." He made a sad face as he murmured, "And me. All alone and forlorn because the one woman I want to spend the evening with turned me down flat."

Had she actually thought he wasn't a sweet-talker? My goodness, he could entice a nun out of her habit! "Okay, I'll go," she acquiesced. Blade's smug expression forced her to add, "But I'm only agreeing to a cookout, nothing more. Understood?"

He held up both hands in mock surrender. "Understood." He gently pushed her backwards and stood, too, towering over her and making her feel small and vulnerable. He was so large. If he ever thought to force her, no amount of training in the world would be able to stop him from having what he wanted. She trembled.

Blade's smile dropped. "Candy?" She only stared at him,

unable to speak. "Sweetheart, it's just me. I would never hurt you," he whispered. "I would rather cut off my own arm than cause you pain. I swear it."

She knew that, she really did. The Vaughn family was all about principle and honor. Candice had gotten to know Merrick through Chloe, and Lacey as well, from having her as her personal trainer. She did trust Blade, but he was still a man, and that irrefutable fact made her uncomfortable. "I'm sorry, Blade. It's not you." She shrugged, angry for feeling so weak. "I guess I'm not ready yet."

Blade touched her cheek with his palm. "Don't back out on me, Candy. Go to the cookout. Let's start with that, then if you're still uncomfortable around me, I'll understand." He dropped his hands, clenched them into fists at his sides, and admitted, "I'll hate it like hell, because I want you. I refuse to lie to you about that. I want you like crazy, and I have for a long time, but I will respect your decision. Understood?"

She blinked then blinked again. He wanted her. Wow, now that was a lot to think about. What would it be like to make love to him in real life instead of just in her dreams?

In her dream world, Blade was virile and possessive and sweet, everything a man should be. How different would the real-life Blade be, Candice wondered, suddenly feeling warm and uncomfortable.

Oh my, he really was something. So dark and hard, and his mustache was the sexiest thing she'd ever seen. Especially when he smiled. A surge of feminine awareness flowed through her. How bad could a cookout be? She would be among people she knew. People she liked and respected. Maybe this was just what she needed. And just what her doctor had ordered.

"Okay, what time should I be there?" she asked as excitement raced through her.

Blade smiled and shook his head. "I don't think so. I pick up my dates, sweetheart, and I'll be here at six o'clock."

He turned and walked to the front door to leave, and she quickly thought to ask, "Wait, what should I wear?"

When he turned back around and raked her body with his bold gaze her insides melted. "What you're wearing now is fine by me, Candy girl."

She plucked at the skirt of her oversized dress. "You like this thing?"

"I thought I made it clear when I told you I wanted you. You could be wearing a brown paper bag and it would be a fucking turn-on."

She had no response to that. Without warning, Blade strode across the room and stood in front of her again. He leaned down and barely touched her lips with his own. The kiss was so quick, only a slight brush of lips, yet its intensity stunned Candice to the core. Then he admitted one more startling bit of information.

"I don't know why, or how, and I swear it's never happened like this before, but I have these dreams about you. Hot, uncontrollable dreams, and damn if I don't wake up hard and ready because of them. Because of you." His voice simmered with barely checked passion. "Think about that today. Get used to it. Because eventually I'm going to get you over your fears, and then you and I are going to make those dreams a reality."

When he walked out her front door, Candice imagined Blade lying in bed, naked and wound up, and all because of her. Could it be true they'd both been dreaming about each other? It wasn't possible, was it? Something else flitted through her mind. "Candy girl"? She giggled at the silly nickname. She'd never allowed anyone to call her Candy, much less Candy girl. But coming from Blade it felt...sexy.

જી

Candice had changed, changed and then changed again. She'd tried on several outfits before settling on a pair of low-slung jeans, t-shirt, and clean white sneakers. The shirt was pink and too big, giving her a small sense of security. Now, all she needed was Blade. He was late, and she started to wonder if he'd forgotten about her. Then her doorbell rang and Candice jumped out of her skin.

She ran to the door and called, "Who is it?"

"It's Blade, sweetheart."

He sounded tired. Candice didn't think that boded well for the evening. She quickly undid the locks and tried very hard not to feel excited that he had indeed remembered her.

"You're late," she scolded as she got the door open, but then her eyes widened in alarm when she noticed his face and hands. "Oh my god! What on earth happened to you?"

"Christ, I'm so sorry, Candy. I would have been here sooner but—"

Candice never gave him a chance to finish. She tugged him inside and slammed the door behind him. She surveyed his injured hands and dirt-streaked face. "What happened to your hands, Blade?" They were scraped and bleeding and it made her heart flip just looking at them. His poor, gorgeous hands. "Have you been in some sort of accident?"

"No, baby, nothing like that," he whispered. "We had some trouble with a contrary roof, that's all." He looked her over from head to toe and growled, "Christ, you're a pretty thing."

"Uh, thank you," she replied, then, "A roof?" Mentally, she squashed the excitement skittering through her over his compliment, but she was secretly pleased she'd taken her hair out of the bun she'd worn earlier. She'd finger-combed it and the soft curls fell past her shoulders. Given Blade's reaction, it had been the right move.

He smiled at her. "Yeah, and if you think I'm beat up, then you should see the roof."

A soft gasp escaped her. "You did this to yourself on the job?"

He nodded and leaned heavily against the door. Heck, she knew he was in construction. Blade had his own thriving business, and she'd assumed he worked out of an office in a supervisory capacity, leaving the grueling stuff up to his employees. She should have figured him for the hands-on type.

"If you aren't up to the cookout, I'll understand." She'd be terribly disappointed, but he seemed ready to drop. Instantly, he stood upright with his legs widespread and frowned down at her, as if he hadn't been exhausted just a second ago.

"You trying to wiggle out on me, Candy girl?"

She blushed. "Well, of course not! But you don't appear ready to—"

He silenced her with a touch of his lips. Like the first, this kiss was also fleeting and barely-there. When he rose again, he grinned mischievously. "Oh, I'm ready all right. If you believe nothing else, you can believe that."

She couldn't ignore the double entendre in his words. She sighed, wishing she were also ready, but it was just a little too soon. "Okay, but I insist we clean those cuts first."

He gave his hands a quick inspection and shrugged, as if that sort of damage occurred daily. Well, she certainly didn't like seeing his hands all beat up, and she would only worry about infection if she didn't tend to them right away.

"Come on," she said, both pleased and nervous when he followed behind her. He was always that way, silent but alert. He reminded her of a panther. She led him to her kitchen and showed him where the soap and paper towels were so he could clean his hands first while she went in search of peroxide and bandages. When Candice returned, he was staring into her fridge.

"Uh, Blade?"

"Geez, woman, don't you ever eat?" He waved at the contents of her refrigerator and slammed the door shut. "Your fridge is practically bare, for Christ's sake."

"Of course I eat, Blade Vaughn, but I'm not accustomed to having big, hulking men to feed."

"A fact I'm not real disappointed about, mind you, but that's about to change, isn't it?"

She rolled her eyes at his chauvinistic attitude. "You think I'd cook for you?"

He crossed his arms over his broad chest. "I need to eat, don't I?"

The man was a total throwback. "No wonder Lacey is always having such a hard time with you."

"What's that supposed to mean? What's Lacey been saying about me?"

Side-stepping, Candice said, "Sit down so I can take care of these cuts properly. We're late enough already." When he only stood there, brooding, she changed tactics. "You do want me to go to the cookout with you, don't you?" The steel in his blue eyes narrowed on her, but he sat. Secretly, she smiled. She knew darn well he wasn't used to being ordered about. She'd bet her last dollar that Blade was usually the one who did the ordering.

Candice went to the table, set the first aid supplies down and got started on the worst of the cuts. She stood over him and dabbed a peroxide-soaked cotton ball on his battered palm, cringing when it fizzed. To take her mind off the oozing blood, she answered his earlier question.

"Your sister loves you very much, but that doesn't make her as blind to your faults as you'd like to think."

He snorted. "What faults?"

She nearly laughed at his genuine surprise. "Your arrogance, for one."

"I'm not arrogant. I just know what I'm capable of."

Candice dabbed and, because she was distracted, asked softly, "Is there anything you aren't capable of?"

Immediately she realized what she'd said and could've smacked herself in the head. She hadn't meant to make him think she thought him perfect—even if she did. After all, it was never a good idea to give a man that much pull over you.

"I'm not capable of cooking a decent meal." His playful smile made her forget what she was doing. "So, if you don't feed me, I just may starve, sweetheart."

She wanted to moan over the sexy sound of his voice, the fascinating features of his hard-edged face. "So, maybe I'll cook for you," she conceded, and could easily have smacked him for smiling so broadly over her concession. She ripped open a bandage, slapped it against his wrist and was rewarded by his grunt of pain.

"Oh, gee, did that hurt?" she asked, feigning innocence.

"You're lethal, lady."

"Hmm," she mumbled. She stood straighter, surveying her handiwork, and smiled in satisfaction. "Funny, that's what my self-defense instructor keeps saying, too."

Chapter Four

Okay, so she was willing to cook for him. She could even fix up his wounds after a hard day's work, and she knew self-defense. He could easily fall for a woman with those qualities.

In the fading light of day, he watched as Candice talked in conspiratorial whispers with his sister. The two women stood in the backyard, apart from the boisterous crowd, while he sat at the picnic table only half paying attention to Merrick and Chloe as they yakked about honeymooning in Hawaii.

Every so often, Candice and Lacey would giggle and look his way. Christ almighty, he could just imagine what Lacey was saying about him. Nothing good, most likely.

"Blade, are you even listening to me?"

He realized, belatedly, that Merrick had asked him a question. "What?" Blade asked, still watching Candice.

"I wanted to know if you'd done that bid on the office building downtown."

Was he serious? Work was the furthest thing from his mind. "Uh, well, thing is—"

Merrick shook his head and laughed. "Look at him," he said to Chloe and their parents sitting at the table with them. Nick, Lacey's boyfriend, stood a few feet away cleaning off the grill. "He can't take his eyes off her for five seconds to string two words together, much less think about work," Merrick complained.

"Well, I think it's nice. I like Candice. She's a sweet girl who deserves a good and gentle man like my Blade." That from his mother, as if he weren't sitting right there hearing their every word. Merrick snickered, but Marie Vaughn wasn't through just yet.

"Honestly, have you ever seen your brother like this, Merrick? He does seem quite preoccupied, doesn't he?" Now she sounded worried. What was he, some dolt who couldn't put his pants on straight in the morning? Just because Candy fascinated him, just because the mere thought of her set his blood on fire and turned his body to iron didn't mean he was completely whipped.

Not to be left out of the *let's help Blade with his love-life* crap, Chloe tossed in her two cents. "Candice is a very sweet girl, and such a hard worker, too. She's never late and never complains when she needs to work overtime. I don't know what I'd do without her, that's for sure."

Even though Blade liked what he was hearing about Candice, he was ready to put a stop to their meddling. He wasn't sure what was going to come of his time with her, and until he had a better grasp for where their relationship was headed, he would tolerate no interference. Not from anyone.

He scowled at the lot of them, and in a deceptively distracted tone said, "You know, Mom, I gave Lacey that boutique card and she said to ask Nick when they plan to set a date."

Nick turned around so fast he nearly lost his scrubber. The grimace Nick sent his way was enough to make Blade grin. And as expected, his mother—the pit bull—began bludgeoning Nick with various reasons why it was so important to select the right date.

Merrick laughed and warned about little sisters and payback. At the moment, Blade could care less; he just wanted to get back to watching Candice. As his gaze zeroed in on her once more, she dropped something on the ground. When she bent low to pick it up, her pert ass jutted toward him, causing Blade to clench his hand too tightly around the neck of the beer bottle he held. Damn. He itched to close the distance between them and grab a handful of her sweet curves.

"Blade can handle his own love life, Merrick, leave him be." His dad, Cal Vaughn, did what dads do: toss in a hand whenever needed. "After all, you know as well as any that when a woman wiggles her way in, you aren't always so inclined to shove her back out again."

That got his attention.

Blade glanced over at his father. It was like seeing himself in thirty years. He was still as big and intimidating as ever, but now, holding his mother's hand gently and with a secret smile lighting his normally menacing eyes, he made Blade wish for that same sort of relationship.

Someday, that was. Way, way off in the future. Obviously.

Deciding he'd had enough of Merrick's needling and figuring it was time to put a stop to Lacey's big mouth, Blade dropped his beer bottle on the picnic table, got up and started toward the two women. Unfortunately, his cousin Josh chose that moment to step up to Candice.

Josh slung a careless arm over Lacey. Blade snarled when he started to talk, smile and flirt with Candice. He was the charmer in the family. His boyish charm and easy smile usually made women melt, not to mention the fact he was practically a poet with words. Blade, on the other hand, was none of the above. He could easily see that Candice might find Josh attractive.

The degenerate. Blade would kick his ass for even thinking about hitting on Candice.

"So he actually let you put bandages on his cuts?" he heard Josh say as he approached.

"Oh, Josh, they were awful! You should have seen them. It was as if he'd tangled with a wildcat and lost."

Josh, the idiot, chuckled. "I just bet he did."

Blade glared at his younger cousin when he drew near, which caused Josh to laugh even harder. He was about to tell him to piss off, but Candice turned and stared up at him with such tenderness that it took all the bristle right out of him. He took her hand in his, entwining their fingers as he did, staking a claim for all to see.

For Josh to see.

Josh's eyes held a challenge, which surprised him. Usually, he was the good-natured one, ready when needed, but content to stay in the background. However, the way he stared at Candice made Blade think maybe Josh had designs on her. No way in hell.

"Show them your hands, Blade. I don't think they realize how bad they are," Candice pleaded.

"Yeah, Blade, show us your cuts," Josh taunted, adding his own unwelcome two cents.

Blade's eyes narrowed to slits as he stared at the little shit, wishing he could pound him. "If I didn't want to embarrass Candice right now, I'd shove both my banged-up hands right up your—"

"Blade!" Lacey warned. "You'll make Candice think we're an unruly bunch of hooligans. Now, stop all this silly chest beating, the both of you." Lacey turned to Candice and explained. "It seems you've got both of them turned inside out, hun."

Candice's expressive eyes grew big as her gaze darted from Blade to Josh and back to Blade. She started to stammer and stutter, but Blade hushed her by bending and placing a kiss to their joined fingers. "Don't worry, Candy girl, Josh knows better than to even think of putting a move on you," he murmured against her soft skin. He glared at Josh. "Don't you, cuz?"

Josh crossed his arms over his chest and grinned. "I have no idea what you're talking about."

Blade wanted to wipe the smirk right off his face. Out of the blue, Josh put his hand on Candice's forearm and noted, "I can see right now that you'll be good for my intimidating cousin. He rarely takes care of himself, and when he does, it's only because Aunt Marie had to browbeat him into it. So, for the family, I thank you for bandaging Blade's boo-boos."

Blade stepped forward, pushed beyond his control, but Candice hastily diffused the situation by laughing and holding him firmly by her side. "You're quite welcome, Josh. I was happy to do it."

Blade was dumbfounded, but Josh's wink and slap on the back as he sauntered off let him know he'd been had, big time. He glared at his sister, but she only patted his chest and smiled. "You really had that one coming, Blade," Lacey declared, then she, too, walked away, saying something about finding Nick and leaving early.

"At last, we're alone," Blade groaned. The blush that stole over Candice's soft cheeks pleased him. He angled his head. "So, what do you think of your decision to come here? Was it as daunting as you thought it would be?"

Candice's surprise told him that she'd forgotten all about her fears. He was glad. It was a step in the right direction, as far as he could see.

"I'm having fun, and I'm a little sad about that, to be honest."

Now that wasn't at all what he wanted to hear. "Being with me makes you sad?"

"Oh no!" she clarified, as if appalled he would think such a thing. "I just mean I feel as I've been living behind a huge brick wall for so long and I've missed so much."

Ah, hope springs eternal, Blade thought. "So, maybe the idea of being...intimate with me isn't such a scary idea?" he asked, holding his breath.

She stared at the ground and kicked at the grass with her foot, not speaking.

"Candy?" he pressed, careful not to push, but needing to know where he stood.

"No, it's not so scary," she confessed. Heat flared in her eyes, encouraging him further. "In fact, I wanted to talk to you about that.".

"I'm all ears, sweetheart," Blade said as unfamiliar feelings flooded his body. There'd been lust when he'd first set eyes on Candice. Secretly, in his dreams, he'd burned for her. Now, as she stood shyly readying herself for what she was about to say, his heart squeezed tight. Hell, he was starting to care for her, and they hadn't even gotten past a few quick pecks!

Blade wasn't sure what to make of that revelation.

"I would like to, you know, do some things." She shrugged. "Tonight. That is, if you want to."

Some things. She wanted to do some things. That was good, but Blade needed to clarify *things*. He didn't want to misunderstand her meaning.

Blade tugged on Candice's hand and brought her around to

the side of the house, where they were out of sight of his family and friends. Once he had her alone, Blade let go of her fingers and cupped her chin in his palm, forcing her to meet his gaze. "I think what you want is to start getting used to the idea of being with me. Touching each other, kissing, making out a little. Is that what you're saying, sweetheart?"

She swallowed hard and answered with an eager, "Yes, Blade. I want that very much." When he started to say, "Fucking fantastic idea, let's leave and start immediately!" she stopped him with a breathy, "Because I've been dreaming about you, too."

Blade couldn't think, couldn't move. Her admission added fuel to a fire that was already blazing out of control. "You've dreamed about me?" She bobbed her head and blushed the tiniest bit more. "Like, the wildly erotic kind of stuff, baby?" he asked, more than anxious to hear all about these dreams. She bobbed her head again, causing the fly of his jeans to strain against the hardest friggin' erection he'd ever had.

"Damn, Candy," Blade groaned. "I need to get us out of here, pronto." When he started to move around to the front of the house to his truck, Candice tugged him to a stop. Every muscle went taut, and he worried she was getting cold feet.

"Shouldn't we tell everyone we're leaving?"

"Hell no! I can't walk through a gauntlet of family and friends with a hard-on like this." Inexorably, Candice's gaze moved down his body and landed on his lap. She hastily looked back at him with a mixture of fear and desire in her beautiful eyes.

He touched her cheek with his fingers. "I'm not a teenager, nor am I Lance Markum. I can control myself, Candice." He stroked a callused thumb over her plump lips, enjoying the soft skin. "If you say stop, we stop. No questions. No recriminations.

I promise you that, baby."

He went still, leaving it up to her. Blade wanted Candice bad, but he wasn't going to push her. He would wait. As long as it took, he would wait. When she smiled and nodded, he wanted to explode in triumph. She trusted him, and for Candice that was saying something. He would not disappoint her.

ɞ

Candice hadn't been intimate with a flesh-and-blood man for a year. What if she panicked? What if she was too clumsy to keep a man like Blade interested? She groaned and worried and fidgeted in the seat of Blade's truck as he drove them back to her place.

He'd probably been with countless women. She was positive none of them had their throats close up at the mere thought of sex. But Blade was so careful with her, so easy and gentle to be around. And he'd emphatically promised to stop if she was uncomfortable. Besides she wasn't the vulnerable, naïve woman she'd been with Lance. She could take care of herself now. Jackie thought she was ready, and her defense instructor had told her she was a quick study. Even Lacey had offered her own thumbs-up, saying Blade was a man of his word. If he told her he'd go slow, then she could darn well count on it. The time had come for Candice to believe in herself.

But as they pulled into her drive, all her newfound courage fled. "Blade, I'm not sure about this."

Blade turned in the seat, smiling in that wicked way he had. "Relax, sweetheart. We aren't going in there and getting naked." He looked down at himself and laughed. "Besides I didn't come prepared for sex. We're just going to do some over-the-clothes stuff. Getting used to each other, remember?" She nodded, and Blade's brow quirked up as he whispered, "Next time, if you ask me very nicely, we'll do more."

Just like that, Candice's reservations fled and she found herself once again feeling safe. "I'm sorry." She covered her face and blurted, "I feel like the biggest tease in the world, pulling you back and forth constantly."

Blade pried her hands away from her face. "You're not jerking me around, Candy girl. I knew this was going to take some time. You're worth all the time in the world."

Candice searched Blade's face for signs of frustration, but she found none. He appeared as if he did indeed have all the time in the world. She sighed heavily, glad he wasn't going to push.

Blade opened the truck door and stepped out, telling her to stay put until he could help her down. Candice was in too big a hurry to wait. She had to practically jump to get out of the truck, because it, like him, was huge. Her legs shook so bad up the walk, she stumbled once. Blade's hand at the small of her back steadied her enough to get to the front door. Once inside, she excused herself to go to the bathroom, while he fetched a couple of cold drinks. When she came back, she found Blade on the couch with two ice-cold colas on the end table and his eyes closed.

He'd stretched his long, lean legs out in front of him and his head lay against the back of the couch. Had he fallen asleep? After such a long day and then the cookout, it was selfish to keep him when he should be in bed.

Careful not to disturb him, she sat on the couch next to Blade and watched him in silence. He really was quite handsome, in a roguish pirate sort of way. In the soft light of the small table lamp, his dark hair shone with flecks of silver. It was a little too long by today's standards, and his mustache was a bit shaggy. He had something of a weathered look from all the hours he'd spent working in the sun, and, oh God, he was so very sexy. Candice was thrilled he was with her and not some other woman tonight. If she had to pick a man to help break her out of her self-imposed isolation, Blade Vaughn was one heck of a choice. Maybe another night... A night when he wasn't so beat up and exhausted from work.

She started to wake him and send him on his way when the deep timbre of his voice broke the silence in the dimly lit room. "You're beautiful, Candice. I hope you know that."

He'd been awake! "Why you sneak!" she admonished, trying not to be so glad about it. "You weren't asleep at all, were you?"

Blade grinned good-naturedly. "Actually, I did get tired, sitting on your comfy couch waiting for you to come out of that bathroom." He leaned closer to her. "I thought I'd been abandoned. Like maybe you'd climbed out a window or something," he teased.

Instinctively, Candice inhaled his musky male scent, nearly quivering in anticipation of the evening that was still to come. "Oh," she murmured.

"You weren't thinking of abandoning me were you, Candy girl?" Blade asked, his voice as seductive as a lover's touch and twice as potent.

"Well, you have had a long day, and I was starting to feel very selfish, keeping you awake so late. You should be in bed asleep."

"If I was at home in bed right now, I'd still be kept awake by you," Blade growled. "In fact, a lot of my nights have been pretty restless lately due to unrequited lust."

She blushed at his words, even as honesty forced her to admit, "Maybe not so unrequited. Remember, I told you, I've been dreaming of you, too, Blade."

He gave her a feral, possessive smile. "Yeah, and we'll get to that, I promise. But first, there's this..." He leaned in the rest of the way and kissed her. This time it wasn't so fleeting or barely-there.

The warmth of his lips was everywhere at once, and her body pulsated with pleasure. He was slow, gentle and skilled as he angled his head for better access. Candice didn't know what to do. Her experience with kissing was pretty limited. She'd never felt so inept. Thinking he was going to stop when he moved back a fraction, she moaned.

"Relax, sweetheart, I'm not going anywhere," Blade promised softly. "But you need to loosen up a little for me, okay?" He unclipped his ever-present cell phone, then placed it on the end table next to the forgotten drinks.

She nodded, thrilled to the core that he wasn't giving up on her. Blade settled back against the couch and said, "Come here."

She stared at him as if he'd gone suddenly mental. He smiled indulgently. "I think you'd be more comfortable if you were the one in control. I don't want you to feel smothered by me. If you were on top, able to stop at anytime, it would help you feel at ease."

She was such a silly twit, and Blade was being so sweet, so unhurried. She couldn't resist the allure of his sexy smile, his relaxed demeanor. Candice lingered over him, unsure and awkward until Blade picked her up and adjusted her so she straddled him. Safely tucked onto his lap, he commanded her with gentle words. "That's it. Now, put your arms around me."

Candice happily obeyed him, beyond pleased at the thick ridge pressing into her bottom. Suddenly his lips caressed hers again, and his arms closed around her in a loose embrace. The lazy and gentle touch of lips soon had her wiggling and moaning on his lap. Need rushed in as Candice craved more. Blade growled low in his throat and slipped his tongue against the seam of her lips, seeking entrance. She opened for him, then he was inside the wet heat of her mouth, tasting and driving her insane.

Oh my, he was the man in her dreams, and she was safe in his arms. Candice desperately wanted him in every way a woman could have a man.

Chapter Five

Never in his life had he been accused of being a patient man. Aggressive. Stubborn. Chauvinistic. Intimidating. Yep, all of the above, but never patient. And right now every fiber in his being screamed at him to toss patience to the wolves and get on with it already. Still he held back, suppressed his innate need to control and dominate, and let Candice run the show.

She was such a fiery little thing, he was sure of it, but she would need to strip off her thick layer of fear first. If he rushed her, he'd only risk alarming her. Blade would die before he caused Candice even an ounce of pain.

That didn't help his gonads one bit. As Candice moaned and wriggled, he was ready to explode. His cock responded to her soft ass with bursts of pulsating excitement. All he could do was sit back and let her play. It was killing him. The best things were worth the wait, he reminded himself for the thousandth time. Nevertheless, that shouldn't mean they couldn't move on to the next stage of their torturous activity.

Blade gently released Candice's mouth, absurdly thrilled when she whimpered her dissatisfaction. "Sweetheart, as much as I love kissing you, I think maybe you're ready for more." The heat and desire in her eyes nearly sizzled his mustache. "Will you let me touch you?" he asked with a fair amount of caution. "Only above the clothes...for tonight," he reminded her. When

153

Candice gave him a breathy, "Yes," Blade's cock grew another inch.

Never once straying away from the deep, blue pools of her eyes, Blade rubbed his hands up and down Candice's back, stroking her taut muscles. She arched for him and he let his hands move around to the front of her. Careful to make sure he stayed on neutral ground, he flattened one palm over her concave belly, delighted when she trembled. She was so small that his hand was able to cover the entire width of her. Christ, she was so fragile, it made him want to protect her from all the evils of the world.

Blade moved his palms slowly upward, ever watchful of signs of panic or fear. When her head fell back and her eyes closed, a wave of tender affection overtook him.

"I'm going to touch your breasts now," he told her softly. Her whimper urged him on.

His hands spread over the gentle swell of her tits and Blade knew a whole new form of bliss. For a man who thought he'd known everything there was to know about women and sexual gratification, it was humbling and thrilling to find out that a slip of a woman could bring him to new heights of pleasure.

"I like that, Blade," Candice rasped out.

"Me, too, baby," Blade assured, as he palmed her. He loved the incoherent sounds she made as he kneaded and fondled. When he took a chance and squeezed her erect nipples between his fingers, she fairly jumped.

"I want you, Candice," he growled, "so fucking bad."

Her gaze fastened on the erection straining against the confines of his jeans. "I will keep my word to you, sweetheart," he reassured her. "Just over the clothes. But I won't lie to you, either. I want to be buried inside of you, so deep and so tight." Blade had to swallow hard to get himself under control. "You'll fit me perfectly, too, I just know you'll fit me perfectly, baby."

"Oh, Blade."

He clenched his jaw and closed his eyes against the need in her voice. It was agony to see her so turned-on, yet unable to do a thing about it. Her next words had his heart racing out of control and made his blood run fast and hot.

"Maybe, we can move under the clothes."

Blade's eyes flew open as he tried to comprehend her words. "Under?" Blade asked optimistically.

Candice nodded, and Blade drowned in the deep blue of her eyes.

"Are you sure?" She nodded again, more enthusiastic this time, and he nearly came in his pants.

"Just tell me what you want and it's yours, Candy. Anything. Christ, everything!" he promised heatedly.

She smiled and, in a voice so soft he had to strain to hear, asked, "Will you take off your shirt? I'd like to see you."

The delicate pleading drove him wild. He wanted to give her whatever she wanted, but he'd made her a promise. Damn it. "I swore only above the clothes. I don't want to break that promise, baby," Blade ground out. Being a man of honor was a nuisance at times.

"I know, and you've stuck to your word wonderfully." Candice's eyes and smile were tender. "But, I think I've waited too long to move on with my life. You've helped me to see that." She touched her hand to his cheek. "I want to know what it's like to feel passion and I want you to be the one to show me, Blade. Please don't deny me."

Hearing her say it, and knowing he wasn't pushing her into anything, helped him make up his mind. Without further delay, Blade whipped his t-shirt over his head and waited. Her gaze traveled over his chest in a heated caress, turning him on further. "Now, will you take off your shirt, Candy girl?" he asked on a ragged breath. "I'd very much like to see you, too."

Candice's eyes grew big. For a suspended moment in time, Blade feared he'd lost her, that he'd gone too far. But then she surprised the hell out of him and whipped her own shirt over her head. She sat straddling his thighs with an unadorned white bra covering her small, pert breasts.

Blade's mouth watered.

He'd never encountered such genuine innocence. She couldn't have been more beautiful to him if she were wearing some fancy bit of lace and satin. Never in Blade's life had he felt more like the pillaging bandit. "I want your bra off," he pleaded. "Please, let me."

"Yes, Blade."

With his hands shaking, Blade reached around and undid the clasp, letting the bra fall to her lap. Candice was a small woman, and so her breasts were, too, but to Blade she was perfect. Round and firm and meant for his hands alone. Her taut nipples were enticing dark-mauve cherries surrounded by sweet, creamy fullness. Blade couldn't seem to muster the strength to stop his fingers from reaching out and stroking the gentle slopes. She moaned and wiggled, and he had to clamp down on the clawing need to take her. To make her his.

She was even softer than he'd dreamed—and Blade had dreamed about her a hell of a lot. Nevertheless, nothing could compare to being able to touch her sweet perfection in real life. He could sit in her barely-lit living room, touching Candy for hours and not get bored.

Blade smoothed his palms over and under, rubbing and cuddling, relishing her rapid breaths. Thrilling over the way she kept her hands in her lap, fisting them together, as if she wanted to do the same to him but was too shy to ask.

"Touch me," he demanded. "Put your hands on my chest and feel me with your fingers."

Very gently, she flattened her delicate hands against him. At first, her fingers shook, but soon she sifted them through his chest hair, playing and stroking.

"Can you feel how fast my heart's beating?" he asked. "I'm excited, sweetheart. Yours is doing the same thing for me. I can feel you beneath my palm, baby. Seeing you like this, all open and ready, it makes me want to taste you. Will you let me do that?" If he could have just one taste of Candy, then surely he'd die a happy man.

"Yes, I-I think I'd like that, Blade."

"I swear you'll love it," he promised. He bent forward and tasted her for the first time. Holding her in his embrace, he sucked on her beaded nipple, laving it with his tongue, encouraged when Candice's fingers pulled his hair, holding him firmly against her. Her head fell back and she moaned long and deep.

He lifted away from her slightly, breathing as if he'd run a marathon, and growled, "You taste so fucking good, woman." Then he moved to the other nipple, giving her what she'd asked for—as much passion as he was capable of giving without self-combusting.

"That feels so incredible," she cried. "I want..." Candice let the words drift off, as if unable to express the turmoil his mouth created.

Blade lifted his head. "I know the feeling."

"But I'm not doing anything to you."

He smiled at her naivety. "Are you kidding? I'm ready to explode here. Believe me, seeing you all hot and anxious is definitely doing something to me."

She blinked, wide-eyed, and whispered, "Oh."

He chuckled. "Yeah, Oh." When she blushed and her smile turned slightly wicked, Blade wondered if maybe Candice was ready for more. "Do you think you could handle the next round?" Her hands came up and covered her breasts. Spellbound, Blade watched her rub them as if trying to quell an ache.

"I do want more. I'm just not sure I'm ready to...go all the way, yet."

Damn if that "yet" didn't please him to no end. "Not all the way, but maybe below the belt?"

She laughed. "The next round, below the belt—you seem to like boxing terms, don't you?"

He grinned and shrugged. "I did some boxing. It helped me get through college."

"I didn't know you went to college. I bet you were good, weren't you?"

Blade's brow quirked up playfully. "Yeah, I'm *very* good."

Candice laughed harder this time, and Blade felt a surge of pride for her. She was starting to feel so comfortable with him that she could talk and laugh even with her tits beautifully bare. Which is how he'd like to spend all his time conversing with Candice, Blade thought with masculine delight.

"I like it when you laugh, Candy girl," he admitted. "You have a real pretty smile."

All at once, her cheeks turned pink, and she tried to cross her arms over her chest.

"Don't do that. Don't shy away from me, baby," he told her, then urged her to drop her arms. She did, but she refused to look at him.

"What did I say? One minute you were laughing and excited and ready for me, and the next you're closing me out. Why?"

"He said that, too. He told me I had a pretty smile. I guess it just reminded me of—"

Blade groaned. "I'm not Lance. Don't compare me to that bastard." She flinched, startled by his outburst, but it killed him to think of what Lance Markum had taken from her. It made him feel helpless. "Aw, hell, I'm sorry, sweetheart," he whispered, "but you have to stop making comparisons. I'm not like him. I would never hurt you."

Candice reached out and touched his cheek, his lips, and Blade grabbed at her wrist and held her palm against his mouth for a kiss. He relished the way her pulse jumped and sped up for him. Only for him, he thought, feeling a surge of possessiveness. He never wanted to see her with another man. The very thought made him sick to his stomach. That confused him. He lusted after Candice, even cared about her, but he wasn't ready to get serious. Was he?

"I know you wouldn't hurt me," she confirmed, taking Blade's mind off his disturbing thoughts. "Or I never would have gone to the cookout with you. But I'm bound to be jumpy when something triggers my memory of that horrible night. I can't help it."

"Christ, I know, I know. I just get a little crazy when I think of what he did to you." Candice started to move off his lap, but he held her firm. "And just where do you think you're going?"

Her smile held a hint of sin and her voice turned husky. "You wanted below the belt, didn't you?"

His mind went numb. Maybe that was what happened to a man when all the blood in his body moved south. "Definitely," he growled, his voice rough with need.

Candice left his lap and started to strip off her shoes and

jeans. In quick order she was standing before him wearing only a pair of white cotton panties, plain white socks and a smile.

He was such a fucking goner.

Chapter Six

"I'm dying to see under those panties, sweetheart, but I don't think you want that just yet. Am I right?"

Blade's voice was a rough thread of sound and his entire body seemed to vibrate with sexual tension, and still he stuck to his word and let her decide their next move. "No, I'm not ready for that, but for the first time I do feel like I could be ready...maybe the next time."

Candice wasn't even sure there would be a next time, since she was quite possibly driving the poor man insane with her shy, schoolgirl attitude. Any other man would have given up by now, called her a tease or worse, and left. Not Blade. He was like a dog with a bone, slowly chewing away at the layers of her fear. As she stared at the hunger in his eyes, Candice knew no other experience in her life had prepared her for a man like Blade Vaughn.

He was powerful even while he was being gentle, possessive, though she knew he wouldn't try to push her too hard, and he was the man she'd made love to countless times in her dreams. At that very moment, she had his full attention, as if she were the only woman on earth. It all left her hot and excited and restless.

"Come back over here, Candy girl, you're way too far away," Blade grumbled low as he held out a hand to her.

She fidgeted, worried that once he got his hands on her mostly-nude body he'd not be able to maintain control. Not that she was the type of woman men lost control over, but Lance had soured her on physical pleasure.

At least she thought he had.

"Blade?" Fear blazed through her as she stared at the huge erection straining his fly.

"You can trust me, baby. We made a deal."

The sincerity on his face relieved her. Blade had more than proven he was a man of his word.

Slowly, she walked toward him. As soon as she was within reach, Blade snatched her off her feet and sat her in his lap again. He groaned and pressed his face to her naked breasts, and Candice's worries slipped away with the first contact of his tongue to her nipple.

It was incredible that a single touch from him could make her feel so many sensations at once, and in so many places at the same time. Her limited experience with men even before the incident with Lance hadn't come close to the way Blade made her feel.

He nibbled and sucked at her as if he had the rest of his life to sit and amuse himself with her body. He sat back, smiling. "You are the most amazing woman."

"No, I'm not." She clasped her hands together in her lap and tried to concentrate on something other than the hard length of him pressing insistently into her bottom. "You've been with countless women. I'm sure there were others that left you feeling much more amazed."

"Yeah, baby, I've been with plenty of women," Blade whispered, "but I've never dreamed of any of them. And they damn sure never had me crazy with lust the way I've been with you."

She liked that she made him crazy, because she'd definitely been going slightly nuts herself. And since he was being so obliging...

"Blade, I'd be much more comfortable if you took off your jeans, too. I feel sort of funny here."

Without a word, Blade lifted her and sat her on the couch, then stood in front of her. He had his jeans undone and pushed down his long, heavily-muscled legs before she could blink. Candice stared, engrossed in Blade's striptease. He wore a pair of tight black boxer-briefs. She could see the entire veined length of his penis. He was magnificent. And huge. He was so masculine and so strong all over. It took her breath away.

The bulky material of his jeans bunching around his ankles forced Blade to sit back down, interrupting her show. He pulled off his work-boots, yanked at his jeans, then he was free. Blade picked Candice up again and plopped her down on top of him, as if there weren't a few measly bits of cotton separating their lower halves.

Candice could feel every rigid inch of him. He may as well have been naked. The hair on Blade's thighs tickled her, and his throbbing erection pushed into her body. It was erotic and sensual and her panties grew moist.

"Better?" Blade asked with a flirty smile playing at the corners of his mouth. Candice nodded, then wiggled around. Blade's carnal moan vibrated to her core. She wanted to give Blade pleasure, to give him something to come back for later. She was on fire, and it was clear that he was, too. But she didn't have a clue as to how to douse the fire raging between them.

"I want..." She stopped, not sure what to say. "To be honest, I'm not sure what I want, which is pathetic for a twenty-five year old woman. I only know I've never felt this way before.

Never."

"Good," he ground out as he slid farther down the couch. He may as well have been lying down, the way he was sprawled. Candice shook her head, trying hard to stay on track—and on top. "It's not good, it's bad. I have no idea what to do here."

Blade's smile was full of tenderness as he cupped her chin in his palm. "I can make you feel good, Candice, and I won't have to remove your panties to do it, either." She bit at her lower lip, still afraid. "Let me take the edge off for you, sweetheart," he coaxed.

"Yes," she uttered, breathless. Blade started moving, clutching her hips and sliding his hips upward, pressing into her sex, then back down again. Candice could feel his cock between her labia. When he pushed into her again, deliberately rubbing the head of his cock against her already swollen clitoris, she whimpered.

"That's it. Just close your eyes and move with me."

Candice obeyed Blade's erotic request. Allowing her eyes to drift shut, she rubbed her lower body against his. Their underwear provided little protection, and yet it was entirely too much of a barrier. She had the wild need to feel his hard, smooth cock inside her. She'd had dreams of it, and now she wanted those dreams realized. She held back, torn between her old need to be on guard and her newly insatiable desire to experience every wonderful inch of Blade Vaughn.

In one swift move, he levered himself up and crushed his muscled chest against her breasts, catching her in a tight embrace. He nuzzled her neck, suckling and biting as if he were marking her. Electricity shot through her. She grew frantic, undulating against Blade's hot, hard body, seeking something just out of reach.

Blade groaned her name, then without any warning, the

beginnings of a climax ensnared her. Her scream came from somewhere deep as she gave herself over to passion.

"Give it to me, baby," he demanded. He stroked his fingers over her clit, plying her through her panties, and Candice went wild.

"Yes, Blade! Oh, god, please!" she shouted, then she was there, flying apart in his strong, capable arms.

"Fuck, baby, me, too," he growled, as his body went rigid beneath her. Happier than she'd ever been, Candice held Blade tight as his body bucked wildly against hers. It was as if they were of one mind, soaring over that invisible edge together. It was beautiful and thrilling and Candice couldn't believe they'd never even removed their underwear.

If he was this lethal clothed, what would he be like unclothed?

Long minutes passed before Blade could even think about moving. Coming in his boxers? Not the way to wow your woman, he thought miserably. Then again, his dick had been on high alert for months now. Since he'd seen the shy beauty, he'd been walking around semi-erect. He was way the hell overdue. Blade hoped he could convince Candice that the next time would be better. He'd be able to hold out longer, make it last. This time was a fluke. Obviously.

Blade sat back against the couch, taking Candice's pliant body with him. He smiled. She'd worn herself out with her fast, fierce ride. He stroked the dampened skin of her back and she stiffened.

"Don't tense up on me, sweetheart," he warned softly.

Candice rose to stare at him, her face a mix of worry and excitement. It made Blade hot just looking at her. "I need to go get cleaned up, but when I'm done we'll talk, okay?"

She smiled at him and moved to get up. Blade couldn't take his eyes off her. She pulled her shirt back on, sans the bra this time, which pleased the hell out of him. A flush rose up her neck to color her cheeks. When she bent to retrieve her jeans, Blade stopped her with a hand on her arm.

"Wait," he demanded. She hesitated, her eyes widening in confusion. "You're so sexy right now with your body all warm and flushed." Like a laser beam, his gaze sought the apex of her thighs. He ached to cup her there, to make her promise she would be his and only his. It was a crazy notion.

"I can see your swollen clit through your panties." He stroked one finger over it then pressed between her fleshy folds, pleased when her body quaked a little. "I promise, one of these days very soon, I am going to taste you." He stared at her mound and rumbled, "I'll bet your pussy is as sweet as honey, too."

She swallowed and her eyes turned dark with arousal. She was in as bad shape as he was; she just didn't quite know what to do about it. Blade was dying to show her what her small, perky body was capable of.

He left the couch and stood over her. "I'll be right back." He bent and kissed her on the lips. Not quite the spot he wanted to kiss, but it'd do for now. Blade grabbed his own jeans and went in search of her bathroom, anxious to clean up so he could get back to the enigma that was Candice Warner.

Chapter Seven

Candice stared at Blade's massive back as he left the room. He had no idea where her bathroom was, and she really should tell him, but she couldn't quite take her gaze off his delicious backside long enough to get her mouth to work. Good Lord, the man was in excellent shape. Even his butt was muscular.

She chuckled at that bit of silliness, then stopped and wondered at the sound of her own laughter. She hadn't felt this good in a long time. She had Blade to thank for that. Lord in heaven, Candice couldn't believe what she'd just done. Sure, it was a far cry from getting naked, hot and sweaty. But for the first time in a while, she wouldn't have to rely on her dreams to get her through the next day. Candice had something real this time. Then a thought occurred. Was Blade thinking of spending the night? She hoped so. It would be nice to lie in his arms all night, hearing him breathe, feeling his heartbeat beneath her cheek. She sighed and tore herself out of her romanticisms, then bent and picked up her jeans. As she was about to pull them on, Blade's words came back to her. He didn't want her to get dressed yet. "What the heck," she exclaimed, feeling decadent as she tossed her jeans on the chair. She grabbed up the sweating glasses of cola and went to the kitchen in search of fresh drinks.

As she opened the refrigerator, Candice heard the soft

rumble of thunder outside. Lightning split the sky and lit the room. A thunderstorm. She stood motionless, holding the refrigerator door open when she heard the first spattering of rain against the windows. She hated storms. Her parents had died in a storm. Most times storms didn't bother her, but on random nights they made her sad. Her parents had had the happiness she felt with Blade and then lost everything with no warning. It didn't seem fair.

She closed the refrigerator and covered her face, holding back tears. She'd lost so much in one swift twist of fate. She wouldn't cry, not tonight, not when everything was so perfect. Candice vowed she wouldn't squander her newfound happiness over something she couldn't change.

Blade found her like that, her shoulders bowed, face in her hands, and it made her sick that he should see her so weak twice in one day.

"Candice?" Blade coaxed gently, touching her shoulder from behind.

Candice swiped at her face and turned to see the tender worry on Blade's chiseled features. She didn't want him worrying over her. She wanted him to see her as a strong and capable adult, not a child who needed to be coddled and protected. "I'm sorry," she said in a soft voice.

"Did I do something wrong, sweetheart?" he asked, clearly troubled that her sadness was somehow his fault.

"No, of course not," she assured him. "Storms bother me, that's all. It was raining the night my parents died. The memories are a little hard to take sometimes."

"I'm so sorry."

The sincerity in his voice soothed her. "Every once in awhile, when I'm at work, I'll catch myself reaching for the phone to call my mom and ask if she's free for lunch."

"Next time that happens you can call me if you want."

She touched his cheek. "I'd love that, Blade."

Blade leaned down and caressed her lips with his. The gentle pressure eased her tension and brought her back to the wonderful here-and-now. Her heart beat too fast, and she tried to calm her raging hormones. He took her hand from his face and placed kisses along her fingertips.

Unable to help herself, Candice stroked his mustache. She'd always loved Blade's mustache. It made him even sexier, a little rough around the edges.

"You like my mustache or would you rather I shave it?"

Blade's voice had gone soft as silk. He kissed his way up her arm and lingered at the crook of her elbow, licking at her there. Candice's legs grew heavy and her body responded to his heated touch.

"What?" she mumbled, not able to concentrate on his words when his tongue kept dancing along her pulse points.

Blade's gaze darted to hers and his smile turned predatory. "I asked if you liked my mustache, Candy girl. Most women want me to shave it. Usually my answer is no to that question, but for you, I'd make an exception."

Her eyes grew big at the horrible notion. "Why on earth would you shave it? It's so sexy and just so..." The thought trailed off. Candice wasn't very good at putting her emotions into words.

Blade looked away from her face, apparently satisfied with her answer, and went back to nibbling on her flesh. He reached her shirtsleeve and frowned. "I want you naked, baby. I want you so bad I hurt from it."

He did sound as if he was in pain, and that wasn't at all what Candice wanted. "But, you just... I mean—"

Blade chuckled. "You mean because I came in my boxers?" Candice closed her eyes, mortified and aroused at the same time, then nodded. "All that did was take the edge off. Believe me when I say if you were willing right now, I would have you on this kitchen floor and be inside you before you could blink those pretty blues at me."

Candice looked down at the white and tan linoleum, then back up at Blade. His face was hard to read, but he seemed to be steeling himself against her rejection. Again. What if she didn't want to reject him? It was time. Time to put the past to rest, once and for all.

Forcing herself to be brave, Candice reached between their bodies and cupped Blade through his jeans. His eyes widened in shock, and she was ready to cheer when he hardened even more under her hand. It was an awesome feeling having Blade Vaughn all hot and excited.

"I want you, too, Blade," she said on a soft sigh. "I told you I've been having dreams, but what I didn't say is that they're wet dreams. Dreams of you and me, and I wake hot and needy. I would very much like to know if you're as wonderful in real life as you are in my dreams." She smiled at the intensity in his eyes. "Will you make love to me?" she asked, and then for good measure, Candice added, "Pretty please?"

"God, yes, sweetheart," he groaned. "But are you sure? I don't want to push you. This is our first date. I can take you out again. We could go to the movies or something. Besides, I didn't bring any protection."

Blade was still being the gallant knight. She loved that about him. Candice allowed her hand to stroke his length and marveled at the way he grew and expanded even more. "I'm positive, and I'm not being pushed. Just so you know, I'm on the pill, have been since I was a teenager, and I've got a clean bill of health. I want you, and I really don't want to wait for a second date to have you."

"I'm clean too. I never go without protection and I get checked regularly. But I didn't want to be tempted tonight." He bent, lifted her into his arms, and carried her out of the kitchen. "I'm real glad you're on the pill."

"Me, too."

"Where's your bedroom?"

Candice cuddled closer to him, enjoying the way his chest hair tickled her cheek, and attempted to answer him without sounding all breathless. "Down the hall. Last room on the right." She could feel Blade's strong arms under her bare thighs and wondered how someone with so much strength could be so gentle. She knew now it wasn't a man's strength that made him mean, but his attitude. Blade had a tender, loving way about him. He could be hard and unyielding if he wanted to be, but intuition told her he would never harm her. Knowing that made it easier for her to surrender.

Blade was close to exploding by the time he reached the bedroom. He carried her straight to the bed and carefully laid her down on top of the plush, dark comforter, ever aware of her fear of intimacy. He located the light switch on a lamp next to her bed and flipped it. Soft white light filled the room. Wearing only her pink t-shirt and white panties and those adorable bobby socks, Candice's small, fragile body against the hunter green of the huge bed had devastating effects on his erection. The sweet, tempting sight of her made Blade want to kill Markum all over again.

With his bare hands.

Slowly.

Making him pray for death.

Blade willed his body to stay calm, pushing thoughts of

Lance Markum to the back of his mind, and instead brought forth visions of what he was about to do with Candice. He needed to be easy with her, to fill her with exquisite pleasure. He couldn't very well come at her like a rutting buck, not after what she'd been through. Blade wanted to prove to her that loving was a sweet—sometimes intense—affair, and always a thing to be cherished. Never degrading or humiliating. He wanted to break down her barriers, force her to toss her inhibitions to the curb, but he knew he'd get nowhere if he didn't tread carefully. As it was, she was already shaking with nervous tension, and that wasn't at all what he wanted. Blade wanted her shaking with passion, not fear.

With her pleasure paramount in his mind, Blade unbuttoned and unzipped his jeans, then pushed them down his legs. Fully aware he had no underwear on—he'd had to toss them after his pathetic loss of control on the couch—Blade watched as Candice saw his cock for the first time. Her pretty blue eyes turned heavy with arousal and her mouth opened into an enticing "O". If he didn't miss his guess, Blade would say she liked what she saw. And he liked that she liked.

He yanked and tossed his jeans aside, then lowered himself to the floor until he was eye level with her smooth thighs. The position put his cock out of her line of sight, for now. He leaned his elbows onto the bed and kept her snared in his sights while he gently pried her legs wide. She was reluctant at first and Blade could feel her thigh muscles trembling, but after some gentle tugging, she relented. He moved them apart as far as they would go, then let his gaze drift over her from head to toe. He wanted her spread like a fucking banquet, appeasing his hungry touch and taste. His gaze took in her pussy, still hidden from his view by her cotton panties, and he frowned.

"I want these off," Blade demanded as he clutched them in his hands at either side of her hips. At the last second, he asked, "May I?" Candice eagerly bobbed her head, as if too frenzied with desire to speak. Yeah, Blade knew that feeling well.

With one quick tug, he tore her panties in two. The startled sounds she made had him shushing her and smoothing his hands over her creamy hips and thighs. Transfixed by the full nest of curls covering her glistening pussy, he murmured, "I won't hurt you, Candy girl, but sometimes sex can be...rough."

Blade reached out and massaged her ribs and belly to calm her. She was so fucking sexy. He was having a hard time not jumping her bones.

His voice was hoarse as he explained, "With the right person, with me, it will only ever feel good, never bad, sweetheart. You have my word of honor."

Blade hoped like hell he could stick to his word. He had vowed to give her pleasure and lots of it, but he needed control. Diving into Lake Erie on a chilly October evening ought to do the trick, but unfortunately, both the lake and October were a long way off. He'd need to rely on good old-fashioned self-control. No problem.

Her eyelashes drifted closed as his palm began to massage her soft skin, barely grazing the underside of her plump breast. Then, teasingly, Blade skimmed down again, not allowing himself to cup the firm globes. Candice whimpered and her body quivered. Her responsiveness pleased him. She had the ability to draw forth every primitive instinct he possessed, even while she had his balls in the palms of her dainty hands without even so much as blinking her dark lashes. Did she have any idea of the power she held over him?

Blade lightly touched the hair of her mound, his feelings rioting out of control. Just once he wanted to see Candice lose it. He wanted her to know what he'd been going through ever since seeing her at his brother's office. Walking around, cocked and ready for that one specific person to yell "fire" hadn't been the most pleasant of feelings. And for some damnable reason, only Candice could set things right. Only she held the magical key that would give him peace. Tonight, he'd bury himself deep and have her in so many ways that by the time they parted company, he'd be well and fully sated of Candice Warner.

He cupped the soft down of her curls, luxuriating in the fact that he was finally able to. That he literally held her pleasure in his hand gave Blade a shot of pure male possessiveness.

"Do you want this with me, sweetheart?" he asked. Her eyes darted open. He pinned her in place with the heat of his steel gaze. "Do you want everything? Because that's what I'm offering. I can't do this half-assed. I need it all or nothing."

"I do want this with you, but I-I'm nervous."

Candice's voice was so thin and small, Blade had to strain to hear. The fear in her voice helped him to stay in check, to remember she needed loving, not ravishment. She needed to know a man in the most intimate of ways, but she had no clue how to go about it. She was innocent and naïve. Any man would be lucky to have a woman so giving and trusting in his bed. That he was that man had Blade flushing with warmth and pride.

"That makes two of us, baby." It was nothing short of the truth. He'd never been nervous with a woman. She wasn't just any woman, though. This was Candy, and he wanted badly do this right.

Her eyes registered disbelief, compelling Blade to prove his point. Holding his hand palm up, he admitted, "I'm trembling like a lost pup here."

She reached out and took his hand in her own, then

brought it to her mouth and placed a tender kiss to each of the spots she'd bandaged earlier. Emotions threatened to overwhelm Blade.

Her curls covering her from his view shone invitingly in the soft light created by the lamp. He could just barely make out her pink clitoris. She was all soft and swollen and incredibly feminine. Suddenly, as if he were willing it to happen, a small drop of moisture trickled out.

He lowered his head, helpless to deny himself a small taste of her tangy juice, and lapped up the solitary drop of dew. He grew so hard and thick, he thought he'd burst. Blade touched her smooth slit with his tongue, and she moaned his name. Candice's legs started to come together as if to stop the sensations rioting through her body, but he captured both silky thighs in his callused hands and pulled them apart again. Blade held them firm while he nibbled her clit and sucked her as if she were a ripe peach. She tasted every bit as sweet as he'd imagined. Blade swiftly became an addict. Candice's barely-there womanly scent and dewy heat was enough to drive him right over the edge.

He would never be able to get enough. With her wild brown hair and tight, perky body, Candice was tailor-made for him. From his position on the floor, he used his fingers to hold her slick, swollen lips open for another lick. She was starting to let herself go, moving against his face and arching off the bed as if she couldn't quite control her own actions. He loved seeing her so wild, her worries and fears abandoned as she gave him what he wanted. Pure, uninhibited passion. She was so beautiful. More beautiful than a rugged construction worker deserved.

Blade let go of one of her sleekly muscled thighs, pleased when she didn't try to close them again, then continued to ply her with his tongue, swirling and circling her distended clit. He managed to slip a single finger into her opening, but Christ

175

almighty, she was tight. Too tight. He was terrified that no matter what he did, no matter how long he took to ready her for the invasion of his cock, she'd still feel discomfort. He could never live knowing he'd hurt her, even in the midst of pleasure. He would have to be even more careful than he'd first suspected.

Gentle as he could be, Blade eased inside her narrow passage, slowly moving in and out as he watched her face for any signs of distress or panic. All he saw was his sweet Candy, completely lost to the torrent of feelings he elicited. The notion that no other man had ever made Candice moan and writhe in ecstasy gave him a predatory feeling he'd never known before.

He moved farther inside her sweet little pussy. Candice's body gripped him, sucked his finger in even more so there was a torturous kind of suction when he brought it out again. Over and over, Blade used his finger and mouth, giving her everything she deserved. Careful, ever mindful of her fear, Blade inched another finger in, watching for signs of pain. But there was only his sweet lover, moaning and arching to press more fully against him, eager and lost to her mounting desire.

Blade growled low and clutched her leg. Digging his fingers into her creamy flesh, he pulled her wider still. He imagined his cock feeling that hot squeeze of inner muscles.

The minute his second finger was all the way in, Blade sucked on her clit one more time. Candice slammed against his hungry mouth and exploded, screaming his name over and over. It was the sweetest sound he'd ever heard.

Blade kept his fingers and mouth on her and inside her until the last of her spasms abated, sucking in every drop of her tangy flavor. At last, he did as he'd wanted to do earlier: Blade kissed her fleshy opening, then rose to look down at her.

Candice's entire body was relaxed. A small smile curved her

pretty lips. Her breasts heaved. She appeared completely and thoroughly depleted. But Blade was far from finished with his feast.

He'd only just begun.

Chapter Eight

Candice had never felt so delicious. She loved the way Blade used his tongue. She loved how he got that fierce look in his eyes when he saw what he wanted—and he wanted her. She loved the way he could be utterly gentle and yet demanding at the same time. She loved...him.

Oh, God, that couldn't be right. Could it? Tears sprang to her eyes. Embarrassed by her outburst, but helpless to stop it, Candice covered her eyes and wept.

Blade was there in a heartbeat, lying on the bed beside her and taking her into his strong arms. He kissed the top of her head and gave her time to settle her frazzled nerves.

She wasn't sure how long she'd lain there, completely engulfed in Blade's embrace while she blubbered like an imbecile. Once she was more in control, Candice pulled back enough to see Blade's hard-edged face. His thick erection pressed against her thigh, only a few scant inches from her throbbing, wet center. Poor man. So far, all he'd done was give her pleasure. She'd been plenty greedy, too. A blush stole over her when he kissed her forehead, as if he had all the time in the world. God, he was simply too good to be real!

"Thank you, Blade," Candice whispered.

Blade cleared his throat and pulled her in tighter. "No problem, sweetheart." His sincere response had her going warm all over. The caution in his eyes as he stared at her gave her pause. It was as if he were trying to decide how best to approach a jittery colt. In the end, he opted to get right to the point, in typical Blade Vaughn style.

"Why the waterworks all of a sudden?"

Candice couldn't have stopped the laugh that bubbled up for anything in the world. Just that quick, Blade's patience seemed to snap.

His blue eyes were devoid of emotion. Immediately, Candice wanted the warmth back. She didn't much care for that somber expression that had his lips thinning into a determined line.

"We don't go any further until I know what the hell I did to make you cry, baby. Not one step further."

"What *you* did?"

His eyes hooded, as if he were steeling himself against some kind of insult. "I don't see anyone else here, do you?"

She laughed. "Of course not, silly, but you didn't do anything wrong, Blade. You were perfect." She hesitated, then explained, "I never knew sex could be like this, that's all."

He seemed to relax. Until that instant, Candice hadn't realized he'd been holding himself so rigid.

A lascivious smile played at the corners of his mouth as he whispered, "Tears of happiness I can handle. It's the other kind that make me weak in the knees."

"You could never be weak. You're so big and strong and everything a woman could want in a man."

Blade's expression turned feral and serious once more. "I go weak when I look at you, sweetheart." He rose over her and pinned her to the bed. "You're my Achilles' heel," he admitted, then he kissed her.

The kiss was hard and unyielding, demanding entrance to

the dark allure of her mouth. Candice was helpless to the sensual assault. She sighed and parted her lips. Blade was there in an instant, taking the advantage, sinking his tongue deep and tasting every savory inch of her mouth. She was drowning all over again.

Oh my, she really had fallen in love with Blade Vaughn. Before she had time to consider all the ramifications of such an enormous mistake, he pulled her up and gently tugged her shirt over her head. Candice allowed him to undress her. It was a unique form of foreplay for her. Her body tingled with twinges of excitement as Blade's gaze devoured the sight of her nude body.

She would need to give the love thing some more consideration. Definitely. But later. Way later. When she didn't have Blade's strong fingers caressing the sides of her breasts and creating a blazing path to her hips. So gloriously strong and yet so gentle. Candice went dizzy as his fingers found their way over her buttocks. He squeezed and kneaded, turning her bones to liquid.

"Blade, please, I want you. I really, really do."

He rose off her, and she was afraid he was leaving her. Candice grabbed him in her desperation to keep him close. She rather liked the weight of him, as if he were surrounding them both in a cocoon of erotic heat.

Blade grinned and patted her bottom once before saying, "I think you'll be more at ease if I'm not crushing you into the mattress, sweetheart."

She could only stare, helpless to the feelings he invoked with his words and strokes.

He nudged her body into the center of the bed and moved to her side. It was odd to have him here, in her sanctuary of sanctuaries. She was glad her panic seemed nonexistent at that particular moment. All she really felt was heady desire. A protective shield seemed to surround her and Blade. As if nothing and no one could hurt them. She liked that idea, maybe a little too much. Candice knew it was an illusion, that the panic could come on at any moment, but for once she didn't feel like a weak coward. She was strong and capable and sexy. She hugged the precious sensation to her heart and chose, for once, to let the past rest. Tonight was for her and Blade.

Braced on his elbow, he hovered over her. For a heated moment, he only stared, then he placed a lingering kiss to the valley between her breasts. As if time didn't matter in the least, Blade spread kisses over both creamy swells. Her breath caught in her throat as he took his time tasting and enjoying her. When he took one hardened nipple between his teeth and lightly bit down, Candice nearly vaulted them both off the bed. Sizzles of electricity zipped through her from head to toe as he nibbled.

He cupped her chin in his palm, forcing her to meet his gaze. "I like the looks of you. I can easily imagine sitting on top of your chest, slipping my cock into your hot little mouth. I'd love to watch you suck me, baby. I've had my fair share of fantasies about that particular love act."

His words turned her on to the point of pain. She was ashamed to admit that while she would gladly take Blade into her mouth, she wasn't sure she wouldn't panic if he were pinning her down. Candice was almost frantic to please him, to leave him with the memory of her as a warm and vibrant woman, not a sniveling baby.

Her thoughts scattered to the wind as his mouth and mustache tickled the soft skin of her needy breasts. He trailed light touches of his lips along the plump undersides, tasting and biting the tender flesh. She instinctively arched, giving him free access. Blade groaned aloud as he insinuated one large, muscular thigh between her legs and used his thigh to massage her core. He cupped her breast firmly in his hand and pulled it up for a long, dizzying suck. His tongue flicked back and forth as he took long, dragging pulls off her.

Candice lost it.

Grabbing handfuls of Blade's thick, dark hair, she held him firmly against her. She was taking no chance that he'd stop his pleasurable ministrations. She closed her eyes, content to let him have his wicked way with her. When he released her with an audible popping sound, Candice's eyes drifted open. The wild need etched into his rugged features made her body burn.

"You have pretty tits. I could easily spend an eternity worshiping them. Still, that jumpy vein in your neck is just begging me to take a bite. May I?"

She could only nod, unsure what he was asking. It didn't matter. She'd give him whatever he wanted. Candice trusted Blade not to hurt her.

He took what she freely offered and lowered his head to the crook of her neck, then kissed his way down until he found just the right spot. Without warning, he bit her. It was the single most erotic thing she'd ever felt. That love bite moved clear to her clit. The light scraping of teeth against soft flesh sent her body into overdrive. When Blade suckled, Candice melted. She shivered and heard herself begging for more. Blade's tongue flicked out and licked the spot he'd bitten. Unbelievably, Candice flew apart for him yet again. Pushing her mound against Blade's hard, hair-roughened thigh, she rode out the orgasm that he'd wrung from her.

Blade smiled down at her, as if reveling in his own success. If she were a fanciful woman, she'd think Blade's possessive and worshipful look actually meant something—that this was more than sex to him. Good thing she wasn't fanciful. Candice stuck to the facts, and the fact of the matter was that her body hummed and vibrated and she knew without a doubt that only Blade had the power to make her come alive.

"I've left my mark on you, Candy girl. Will that bother you?"

She shook her head. "No, it won't bother me." Then in a more controlled voice, Candice confessed, "I-I've never had anyone do that before."

Blade's eyes turned dark with what seemed to be a slightly arrogant sort of masculine delight. "Good."

He removed his leg from between her thighs, but stayed pressed against her side. His gaze roamed over her body as he spread his work-hardened hand over her flesh. Pressing down on her nipples, he massaged little circles over the buds, drawing incoherent moans from deep within Candice.

"You're so beautiful, baby," he praised in a ragged breath, "and I'm so glad you changed your mind."

She trembled, but managed a nod, wholeheartedly agreeing with him on that count. "Me too, Blade. So very glad."

"I want you to look at me, sweetheart, to get accustomed to my body and know I won't hurt you."

She did as he instructed and let her gaze travel over him. He lay so close that she could smell the clean scent of his soap and the musky heat of his skin. It was a delicious combination. He propped himself on one elbow and stared down at her with such reverence it made her hyper-aware of her nudity and all its horrible flaws. Blade didn't seem to notice any of her imperfections.

On the other hand, his perfectly sculpted body and awesome arousal had her squirming. He was so large; it was a little scary to imagine him seated deep inside her. His heavy sac nestled in a thick patch of dark curls. Candice's mouth watered for a taste of Blade's spectacular body. Apprehension was ever-present, but she was curious all the same.

183

She'd never been intimate with a man like this, lying in the soft light, both of them nude and taking their time to discover each other. It wasn't quite as daunting as she'd imagined.

"Do you like what you see?"

She smiled and whispered, "Very much. You're beautiful, Blade."

His eyebrows shot up. "Beautiful?"

"It's true. You have a body that makes a woman think all sorts of naughty thoughts. Surely you must know that."

He looked very much like the cat that ate the canary. "Well, that I can handle. Still, men aren't beautiful, sweetheart," he scolded. "Handsome, hot, sexy, but never beautiful."

She shrugged. "Well, I say you're beautiful."

Blade's gaze made a sensual path down her body, catching on her breasts, then her damp curls at the juncture of her thighs. Suddenly, their silly bantering was over.

"I want you to touch me."

Oh my, she wanted that, too. But if she panicked...she would just die if she panicked. "Blade, I'd like that, I really would, it's just—"

He touched her nipple with a finger, which stopped her rambling. "You don't have to touch my cock, just touch me. Anywhere you want. Hell, everywhere. I'm dying to feel your fingers on my skin, baby."

Blade's voice was tender, but she could hear the desperate longing, too. He was being so patient with her.

"I just want to feel your hands on me," he reiterated when she still didn't move.

It was a good thing Candice's hand had a mind of its own, otherwise they may have stayed like that indefinitely. She reached out and stroked over Blade's solid, powerful chest, then

184

sifted through his dark chest hair and down over his hard abs. God, he had some seriously sexy abdominal muscles. "Abs of Steel" had nothing on Blade Vaughn. Taking them both by surprise, Candice took hold of his jutting cock and squeezed. She was helpless to stop her fingers from curling around him. Powerless to keep her palm from stroking over his thick, silky shaft.

Blade closed his eyes on a groan. "Christ, that feels good."

"You like it?" She was such a novice, not knowing what to do, how to please.

"Damn right, I like it. Your soft hand wrapped around my dick is a pretty major fantasy of mine."

"Oh," she uttered, breathless, her heart pumping out of control. Her body started to react to the way he plucked at her nipple and cupped her breast, squeezing much the same way she squeezed him. She wondered what it would be like to taste him.

"Blade?"

"Yeah, baby?" he gruffly replied.

"Can I lick you?" Candice asked shyly. When his eyes snapped to hers, she quickly added, "You know, like you did me?"

Blade's jaw clenched and unclenched, then he answered with a nearly unintelligible, "Yes."

Candice didn't hesitate. She slithered down the bed until she was eye-level with Blade's cock, then took a moment to admire his male perfection. His bulbous head was swollen purple and the entire length throbbed. Not giving herself a chance to think about it, Candice leaned over him and opened her mouth wide, then sucked as much of his length into her mouth as she could.

A groan rumbled out of Blade, and he cupped the back of her head in a protective hold. When she brought his entire length out and licked him from tip to base, Candice heard him growl, "Fuck, that's all I can take, baby." He pulled her off him, gripped her torso and pushed her to her back.

"Play time's over,," he murmured as he straddled her thighs.

His mouth swooped down on hers in a hot, hungry kiss. Candice wrapped her arms around his neck and kissed him right back with just as much passion and heat. It was frightening how hungry they were for each other. Candice ached all over as desire started to spin out of control.

He deliberately pried open her mouth and delved inside, plundering her. He took nibbles of her lower lip as if she were a noontime snack. Blade licked, she moaned, and both of them shook with need. He intoxicated her. He could do nothing she wouldn't enjoy.

Blade raised his head until he was a mere breath away and devoured the sight of Candice Warner. Her eyes were closed, her lips parted, her tits flushed and trembling. She looked like...sex. Candice pulsated with life, and her body was so fucking lush, Blade couldn't stand taking it slow. She was all that a woman should be, and more.

Her tousled hair and rosy cheeks were the prettiest things Blade had ever seen. Her lips, devoid of any lipstick, were as succulent as ripe peaches. He could eat at them for hours. He'd never be able to slake himself of Candice's sweet honey.

There was something else Blade spotted. His mark. He stared at the purple bruise of his bite on her neck and something inside him snapped. A floodgate opened, and a primal, fiery need to mate came over him.

"Candice." His voice was a scrape of gravel in his throat. Blade sat motionless on top of her and waited until her eyes fluttered open. "Turn over," he demanded.

He rose up on his knees and moved back, allowing her enough space to do as he bid. When she was lying on her stomach, he simply grabbed her waist with both hands and raised her up on her knees. Once she was on all fours, he had a perfect view of her round ass, but her legs pressed shyly together.

"I won't hurt you, baby," he said tenderly as he placed a kiss to her sweet, heart-shaped bottom. "Open for me."

Blade slipped one hand between her thighs, beyond pleased when she spread her knees apart. She was completely exposed to him now. Blade groaned like an animal in pain.

Her pink pussy was swollen and ready. Her pretty, dark pubic hair was a dense, protective covering, as if it defended some precious gem.

God, she was magnificent.

Blade reached out and covered her mound with his hand, cupping her. "Mine," he commanded, and he plunged one finger between her already wet labia. Candice's back arched and she fairly purred. He stroked her inner muscles and felt them tighten around his finger. Even after three orgasms, she was still so responsive. Over and over, Blade stroked, building the fires higher. It wasn't until he reached around her hips and took her clit between his finger and thumb, rolling and squeezing, that Candice flew apart, screaming and bucking against his hands.

As her body came back down to earth, Candice collapsed onto the bed. Blade smiled in triumph. Her body would be a tight, slippery heat now, and he couldn't wait another second to be inside her.

Blade pulled up her bottom, placed a fat feather pillow under her hips so that her ass was in the air, then covered her with his body. Anchoring his arms on either side of her ribcage, he ordered, "Look at me."

When she turned and stared at him, her eyes at half-mast, he reached one hand between their bodies and positioned himself against her entrance. Holding her gaze, Blade slipped slowly into her for the first time. Candice threw her head back and moaned long and deep in a mixture of both pleasure and discomfort.

"It's too much, Blade." She whimpered.

Candice was much too tense, and her inner muscles clamped around him hard. "Just relax for me, baby. You're too nervous." He pushed the heavy fall of her hair out of her face and kissed her cheek. "I need you to calm down. Let's not forget who you're with. It's just me, baby. You trust me, right?"

When she hesitated, Blade moved his lips lower, kissing the long, elegant length of her neck. She liked when he kissed her neck. He'd figured that out real quick. Blade used that knowledge now to take her mind off her fear at having a man inside of her for the first time since her trauma. Blade wanted to erase all thoughts of what Markum had done and replace them with sweet memories of their loving.

He stroked her body and kissed his way over her shoulder blades. Soon she relaxed and arched into him. He pushed inside another inch. Candice squirmed, but this time it was from excitement not discomfort. He lifted her bottom and slipped his hand over her mound, rubbing and stroking her clit. Her body eagerly responded.

Candice wiggled against his groin as if needing more of him. "Do you want the rest of me inside your pussy, baby?" he asked, needing to hear her say it.

"Yes! Please, Blade," she begged.

"Mmm, those are the magic words." He rose, grasped her hips, holding her still for his invasion, then drove into her hard and fast. Blade buried himself deep. "You're so fucking tight, I feel like I've died and gone to heaven."

This was nothing like the slow, easy seduction he'd practiced with her earlier. This time they were both frantic and desperate to slake their lust. It was a hot, hard coupling of two people perfectly suited. Suited, hell. She fit him like a tight fist. It was basic and animalistic, and he practically howled at the moon.

He pushed at her, forcing her further over the edge of sanity, wanting more, always more. He bucked and thrust into her wet heat, harder and harder, until she went wild beneath him.

She threw her head from side to side, and all at once her muscles clenched. In perfect harmony, they both flew up and over, disintegrating into space.

He stayed inside of her for another minute, not willing to let her go. He could never get enough. Blade doubted even a lifetime would be enough. He would always be insatiable where Candice was concerned.

Reluctantly, Blade pulled out of her. Candice had long since collapsed on the bed, totally spent. He got up and went to the bathroom to clean himself. After locating a washrag in a linen closet, he ran warm water over it, then took a minute to grab his cell from the front room before bringing the wet cloth back to Candice.

He dropped his phone on the bedside table and lay down next to her on the bed. He stared at the juncture of her thighs, enraptured by the way his semen seeped from between her soft pink nether lips. Christ, what a pretty sight.

She might be on the pill, but no method was fool proof. What if she ended up pregnant? Blade found himself smiling like an idiot over the idea.

He was such a damned sap.

He tried to dredge up a little self-loathing for his thoughtlessness, but nada. Zip. The thought of Candice round with his baby made him grin, not cringe.

What a dumb ass.

Blade pulled the pillow out from beneath her, then turned her over and started washing away his seed. As he massaged the washcloth over her soft, delicate folds, Candice never moved a muscle. Once he was finished, he dropped the washcloth to the floor next to the bed and scooted her over. She whined like a petulant child. Blade grinned. Poor thing was worn out. He curled his body protectively around hers, then reached down to the foot of the bed and covered them both with the extra blanket that lay there.

For a long while, Blade watched Candice while she slept inside the cradle of his arms. He gently moved her hair away from her face and ran his fingers through the soft mass, loving the silky texture against his skin.

He wondered what she would look like pregnant. Beautiful, no doubt. Her breasts would get full and heavy with milk; her belly would grow big. Jesus, he needed to quit thinking and get some sleep. Tomorrow he would talk to her about protection—or the lack thereof—and deal with it then.

As he let his eyes drift shut, he wondered what she was dreaming about. Him, the way she'd claimed? He hoped so, because she was sure as hell inside his head. Whether he was sleeping, eating, working or showering, it didn't seem to make a difference. She was everywhere all the time, driving him crazy.

For now, however, Candice was here, in his arms, where

she belonged. He had a need to protect her. He couldn't stand the thought of someone hurting her. If she was under the impression that this was just a one night thing, Blade would just have disabuse her of that bullshit notion.

They woke late into the midnight hours and made love two more times, coming together with a lazy kind of sweetness that brought even more rapture than the fast and crazed loving they'd shared earlier. Afterwards, they fell into a deep, lover's sleep, wrapped in each other's arms.

Chapter Nine

Blade woke when Candice started to shuffle out of bed. "Where you going, baby?" he asked in a sleep-roughened voice as he grabbed Candice's arm to halt her escape.

"I need a hot shower." She looked at him a moment, a pretty, content smile lighting her drowsy eyes. "You may be used to all this...activity, but I'm not."

Blade smiled with possessive delight. "Yeah, I know. Pleases the hell out of me, too," he said, starting to get up with her. "Come on, we'll shower together."

"Together?"

Candice sounded scandalized by the idea. Amazing after all they'd done together, she still blushed over the idea of him seeing her wet. He'd never figure out the female mind, not as long as he lived.

"Together," he reiterated, then proceeded to drag her cute, naked body from the room.

"Blade, I'm not entirely sure about this."

She frowned, biting her lip and trying to cover her breasts with her one free hand. Which wasn't really working out too well for her. He stopped in his tracks as a horrible thought occurred.

He lifted her chin with the side of his fist. "Are you sore, baby? Was I too rough?"

Candice's expressive blue eyes grew large. "Oh, Blade, it was wonderful. You were wonderful."

"That doesn't answer my question. Are you sore?" he asked again, with more force this time.

She shrugged and stared down at the floor. "A little."

He was an animal. Scum. The lowest form of scum. "Shit, I should have left you alone after the first time."

Candice quickly shook her head. "Don't you even think it, Blade Vaughn. Every minute, everything you did was worth some soreness this morning."

He stared another second, then visually scanned her. He didn't see any bruises, and considering how vigorous he'd been that was amazing in and of itself.

"I'll wash you," he stated. Candice blushed. Her modesty had him smiling. He moved behind her and kissed the delicate skin below her ear. "Real gentle. It'll feel good, I promise, baby."

Just the idea had his usual morning erection going harder. He seemed to sport a permanent woody around Candice.

Blade gave her a nudge, spellbound as her ass swayed while she moved the rest of the way down the hall. It was a sight he could get used to.

Once in the bathroom, Candice bent and turned on the overhead spray. Blade couldn't resist a quick feel. He reached out and slid two fingers over the silky seam of her bottom, causing her to jump and screech.

"Blade!" she yelped.

He chuckled shamelessly. "Well, you stuck it right out there for me. What's a guy supposed to do? Besides, you do have the sweetest ass, sweetheart." Blade growled.

"Oh."

He chuckled at how naïve she was to her own sex appeal. The woman had set his blood on fire the night before and yet she still acted like a virginal school girl around him.

Blade kissed her forehead, enjoying her more by the minute, then gave her butt a swift swat, ordering, "In you go, Candy girl."

He waited for her to step into the tub before moving in behind her. "Which soap?" he asked, perplexed by the countless bottles that littered every flat surface of the tub.

Candice had about five different scents from what he could tell. What was it about women that they thought they needed to be all smelly? It was the feminine scent they were born with that a man liked best.

"How about this one?" She held up a short, fat bottle with some sort of milky stuff inside.

He popped the top and sniffed for himself. "Mmm, yeah, I like this."

She beamed at him, apparently pleased by his comment. "Milk and Honey. It's my favorite."

"Ah, I see. Well, let's find out what it smells like on, shall we?" he asked with wicked delight.

Washing a woman, washing Candice Warner, would undoubtedly be on his top ten list of favorite things to do.

Blade located a peach-colored puff and squirted some of the milky liquid onto it. He squeezed it, watching the bubbles appear and started on her arms. He moved downward, washing each finger with great care before moving on to her back and finally her feet. She had cute toes. Her middle toe was somewhat crooked, and Blade found it adorable. She giggled, and he looked up from his kneeling position to see her holding back a laugh.

"Ticklish?" he asked with mischievous intent. Candice squinted suspiciously down at him and gave him a petulant shrug.

Seeing that little movement as pure challenge, Blade purposely washed the soles of her feet, loving the laughter that spilled out of her. He kept up his gentle torture until she cried uncle.

Candice was becoming so free with him, it turned his heart to mush. Damn, he was in love with her. It was as plain as the impish nose on Candice's face. An easy sort of contentment washed over him.

He moved up her strong calves, past her knees to her soft thighs. Candice's laughter died, giving way to fast breathing and languorous eyes.

"Spread your legs for me, baby." When she did as he asked, Blade dropped the puff and poured the soap directly into his palms. Nothing was getting in the way of his hand and her flesh. He massaged the white liquid into her mound, stroking her swollen folds and clitoris. As he stared at her there, he saw redness. He was an ass for taking her so many times when she hadn't had sex in so long.

"Mmm, that feels so good, Blade."

He looked up her slim body. Her nipples were erect and her swollen lips were slightly parted. She was all wet from the hot spray and it made him want to drink her in. Blade spent a few more minutes gently rubbing, soothing the soreness away as best he could, then he allowed his fingers free rein.

He squeezed her clit and slipped a finger between her puffy, slick folds. To his wonder, Candice started undulating against him, moving his finger in and out and moaning deep. He pumped at her clit, then pushed another finger inside her wet heat, finding a rhythm that he now knew she liked. When she screamed his name and clutched his shoulders for support, he wanted to fuck her so bad his body ached for it. Blade held back. Knowing how sore she was already kept him in check. He cupped her mound, holding in her pleasure for another second, then kissed her rounded hip before moving to her ass.

"Blade!" Candice squealed when his soapy hands stroked the cleft of her pert ass. It shocked her out of the sleepy aftereffects of her climax.

"All of you, baby," he said in an unrelenting tone. She bit her lip and reluctantly let him caress her. Possessive delight filled him at the idea that she was letting him do things to her that no other man had ever done.

Blade swept his fingers between the firm globes and slicked them back and forth over her puckered opening. His mind imagined his cock where his fingers were. As he inched his pinky inside, Candice stiffened. Blade was careful, gliding in and out, never straying too far. The tight grasp made his mouth water. He was dying to fuck her there, but she wouldn't be ready for something so carnal. Yet.

Once Blade was satisfied with his job, he slipped his finger free and rose to his feet, then commanded in a low whisper, "Now, turn around." She did, and the water ran over the length of her. The sweetly scented bubbles ran down her breasts, her abdomen, until at last she was glistening.

Candice peered over her shoulder at him, a sensual smile curving her tempting mouth. "Your turn," she taunted.

Oh hell. He hadn't figured on that. How was he supposed to keep from sliding deep inside her tight body if she started touching him? He simply didn't have the strength.

"Uh, you don't have to. I'm enjoying the hell out of myself as is."

Candice turned all the way around and her big, pleading

blue eyes nearly did him in. "I'm not suggesting that I have to, Blade, I want to. Badly. Please, don't deny me."

Blade's throat clogged with emotion, giving in to Candice's charming sincerity. "I wouldn't dare, baby."

She reached for the milk and honey soap, then poured it into the puff, but when she started washing him with it, he chuckled.

"Uh, sweetheart?"

"Hmm?" Candice mumbled as she stared at some interesting spot on his arm.

"Real men don't use puffs," he said, amused and turned on by having Candice's undivided attention.

She finally managed to drag her gaze away from his forearm and stared at him as if he'd lost his mind. "You can't be serious?" When he only shrugged, she rolled her eyes. "What does it matter what I use, so long as you're clean?"

"It matters, believe me." Blade knew he sounded absurd but he couldn't help it. It was bad enough he'd let her put bandages on a few measly cuts; if word got out he'd let her use a peach-colored puff and milk-and-honey bath soap he'd never hear the end of it.

A man had to put his foot down somewhere.

"Drop the puff, sweetheart, and just use your hands on me."

Her eyes lit with desire at that, and Blade gave in to a smile. She was becoming quite the glutton, just as he was with her.

Candice hung the puff over the faucet handle and squirted some of the soap into her hands instead. She rubbed them together, then went back to washing his forearms. She moved her delicate fingers up and down, first, one, then the other.

Blade knew he'd have the cleanest arms known to man.

He loved feeling her fingers on him—it was a major turn on no matter the body part—but if she didn't...ah now that was more like it. She'd managed to shift her attention from his arms to his chest. Much better. Now just a bit lower, he thought with a wild kind of anticipation that he couldn't remember ever feeling.

"You are so big, so hard, Blade. Just everywhere." Candice's voice was husky and low, and he knew she was getting herself worked up.

She was beyond her shyness with him now and her panic seemed long gone. Her chest heaved, a sinful smile curved her lips. It fascinated him to watch Candice become increasingly aroused, like a flower opening after a hard spring rain.

An almost overwhelming and possessive need to be inside her filled him. Deep and tight. Where he was home. Where he belonged.

She dropped to her knees in front of him, as if afraid he might disappear if she didn't hurry and touch him. She reached out with both slippery hands and grasped his cock, gripping and stroking, driving all intelligent thought from his mind. Blade had to steady himself on the shower wall when she looked up at him, smiling like a conquering warrior maiden.

"Pretty proud of yourself, aren't you?" he growled.

She answered by cupping his balls and squeezing gently, wringing a moan from deep within. Knowing that Candice was able to have so much free and uninhibited fun with him was enough to make him want to shout to the world that she was all his. He was beyond pleased she'd chosen him to help her emerge from her cocoon.

As soon as their shower was over, Blade was going to get down to the business of finding out just where he stood with her. He wanted to swear his undying love, but he wasn't sure Candice was ready for that much of a commitment from any man, or if she'd even believe his affirmation of love. She'd become accustomed to dealing with things on her own, relying only on herself. That would soon change. She wasn't alone anymore, and Blade wanted to prove to her that she could lean on him.

Apparently done washing his front—an unfortunate turn of events to Blade's way of thinking—Candice moved her hands around to his back, sudsing his feet first. She traveled up his calves, thighs, and then lastly his ass. She paid special attention to his ass. He even thought he heard Candice elicit a throaty moan. Then she sat back and ordered, "Now, turn and rinse."

Demanding little thing all of sudden, Blade thought with glee as his dick grew another inch. What kind of monster had he unleashed anyway? He pondered that while he let the water run over him and then she was commanding him to turn around.

Still on her knees, Candice murmured, "I want to taste you again, Blade. I liked it last night, but you stopped me too soon."

He stood rigid. Mute. Edgy. Ready to pull her up and slam his cock into her wet cunt. While he was still trying to rein in his control, Candice issued yet another order. "Don't stop me this time."

All Blade could do was bob his head before she drew him into the hot cavern of her mouth.

"Damn, baby," Blade bit out between clenched teeth. He grabbed fistfuls of her sopping wet hair and pulled her against him more fully. She moaned and brought her hands up to massage his balls. She was inexperienced enough to drive him crazy, but ardent enough to have him panting and bucking.

Blade held on tight, keeping her from drawing back out again, and began to pulsate against her fondling tongue.

"Suck it, Candy girl," he ordered. When she quickly obeyed, Blade came in a rush of fluid.

When he was able to think again, Blade realized he still held her head against him, with his semi-erect cock in her mouth. Candice's eyes had closed and her arms were around him, holding him in a tight embrace. He smoothed back her hair, then whispered, "I love you, Candice Warner."

Chapter Ten

Candice was in a daze. Love? He'd said he loved her? He was crazy! Of course, there was no way he meant it. Men said those sorts of things all the time in the heat of passion. Didn't they?

They'd finished their shower, Blade took extra care in drying her, and now she was perched buck naked atop her kitchen table while Blade, sitting in the chair between her dangling legs, fed her spoonfuls of frosted flake cereal.

What on earth did she know of love? The only people she'd ever loved were her mother and father, and they'd died. She had no real experience with loving a man. Candice had accepted the fact that what she'd felt for him wasn't just some passing fancy, but she still needed time to think.

The weekend had been a whirlwind of activity for a hermit like her, and now that she'd taken the first step towards her new future, Candice needed to see whether or not she was going to stand or fall. She could only do that on her own. If Blade hovered over her, he'd only keep her off-balance, more than likely in bed, making love. Really, the man was insatiable. He would have her thinking of nothing but sex, which would effectively keep her from thinking of Lance.

"Blade, we have to talk."

"Shh, just eat, we have plenty of time for talking,

sweetheart."

The man was unbelievable! He seemed perfectly content to feed her, as if he hadn't just turned her world upside down with those three little words. Candice needed order, darn it.

"Blade," Candice growled, more fervent this time. He ignored her and attempted to give her another bite, completely oblivious to her growing anger. She reached out and grabbed a handful of his chest hair, then tugged.

"Ow! What'd you do that for?"

"Because you keep ignoring me!" she shouted.

His gaze raked her from head to toe and electricity zinged through her body. "Oh, believe me, all my focus is on you, baby."

She wanted to talk, to be all serious and sophisticated, but the intense heat searing her body tied her tongue into knots. "I want us to discuss what you said in the shower."

"I said I love you. What's the problem?"

"Blade! You can't just say these things and then expect me to not completely freak."

"What's to freak about? It was bound to happen. I can't keep my hands off you. I think about you day and night, and for a construction worker that can be deadly."

He'd started to stroke her naked thighs and arousal bloomed at the feel of his callused hands so close to her mons. *Do not be swayed*, she commanded herself. She stopped his hands as they approached too close to her sex and said, "How on earth do you know it's love? Maybe it's lust, Blade. Infatuation. Something perfectly normal like that."

His mouth quirked into a playful smile. "Lust and infatuation are normal, but not love?"

"Not so fast, no!"

His brows shot up. "So it's your feeling that my parents are just in lust then? Because they met and fell in love pretty much overnight."

He wasn't getting it, and she couldn't help but wonder if that was deliberate. "No, of course not, Blade. It's just that, I need some time. I need to think about this. I'm a mess emotionally. I can't just leap off some cliff into oblivion."

His face hardened, eyes turning cold, and, sadly, he had stopped trying to inch his hands upward. "I see. So, I'm a frightening cliff now. That's how you see me?"

Candice's stomach bottomed out. "Oh, please don't think that." She cupped his face in her hands. "You are without a doubt the best thing that's ever happened to me. Everything you've done, everything *we've* done, has been like a dream come true."

"Then why the hell can't you trust me?" he demanded. "Why are you sending me away? That's what you're doing, isn't it?"

"No!" Candice cried. If she screwed this up, she would lose him. That thought left her feeling more anxious than ever. "But, when you're near me, touching, playing, it's hard to think clear. I need time." His eyes softened a fraction. "I'm barely capable of taking care of myself, and now that I'm in l—" She broke off abruptly, not willing to share her deepest heart's desire with him just yet. He'd steamroll right over her if he realized that she was in love with him, too. She needed time to deal with her past if she was ever to have a future. A future with Blade Vaughn. It sounded sweet. Perfect. Right. Still, none of it would work if she couldn't stand on her own two feet first.

Blade was so quiet, staring at her and not saying a word. It made her nervous and edgy.

She broke the silence, not willing to let him think she was

pushing him out the door like some one-night stand. "I'm only asking for some time alone. A day, maybe two, no more. Just enough time to get my head straight."

He silently watched her, then finally grumbled, "If that's what you want I won't stop you." She wanted to sigh in relief. "But I'm coming back. Soon." He leaned down, placed a possessive kiss on her pussy, then rose. "We'll see then if you still think I'm in lust with you."

&

Candice walked into Jackie's office Monday morning with renewed purpose. It was the first time she'd ever eagerly anticipated an appointment with her therapist. This time, she wasn't coming to tell her how pathetic she was, how scared and lost she always felt. This wasn't going to be like her usual visit. Nope, this time she had something good to report. Something beautiful. Candice smiled and her body heated just thinking of the way she'd left Blade yesterday morning.

He'd been so incredibly wonderful. Such a giving lover, so passionate and gentle. Candice couldn't stop thinking of all the intimate things they'd done together. Attempting to fall asleep in her bed Sunday night had been tough because she could still smell Blade's masculine scent on her sheets and pillow case. She'd lain in the dark, feeling positively surrounded by him, to the point that she'd dreamed of him again. This dream hadn't followed along the usual lines, however. Her dream-Blade was more real now. Solid and powerful and sexy.

Candice had gone asleep imagining him the way he'd left her Sunday morning, feeding her frosted flakes, both of them naked and vibrating from their encounter in the shower. Only, instead of making him leave, she'd let him stay. He'd pushed her backward on the kitchen table and made love to her, body and soul. Candice had woken sweating and throbbing. It had taken a very long, cold shower just to calm her raging hormones enough to get dressed.

Needing to go see her therapist anyway and wanting a day to mull things over, Candice had called in sick as soon as she'd woken. Chloe had been terrific about it, too. It'd been the first time she'd missed work since Merrick had hired her.

"Hi, Mary, I'm here for my ten o'clock."

Mary, Dr. Jackie's trusted secretary, glanced up from her laptop computer and promptly squinted at her. "You look...different."

Candice wasn't the least bit surprised. Every other time she'd come to Jackie's office she'd been woeful and resigned. A smile had never once come into play. But that was before Blade had stormed into her life and made her feel again.

"You're right, Mary, I am different."

Mary slowly smiled at her, giving her the once over. Candice's face heated. She'd decided to be brave and wear something that didn't resemble a tent. Unfortunately, she'd been forced to dig pretty deep into her closet. The pretty yellow sundress she'd found had been worth it, though. The spaghetti straps crisscrossed in the back and the dress hit her just above the knees. The fitted bodice had made her very nervous at first, so nervous in fact that she'd almost gone back to her old baggy jeans and t-shirt. But, she was determined to get her life back on track and the yellow sundress was a step in the right direction.

Squaring her shoulders, Candice asked, "Good different or bad different?" Anxiety rushed through her as she wondered at Mary's answer.

Mary gave her a wink and a nod. "Oh, it's definitely a good

different, hun. You're positively vibrant. Great dress, by the way."

Candice nearly sagged in relief. She hadn't realized how nervous she was over her small transition. Then again, going from frightened mouse to assertive woman was nothing to sneeze at. She clearly had a long row to hoe.

"Go on back, Candice, Dr. Jackie is waiting."

Candice nodded and thanked Mary, then strode down the hall to Dr. Jackie's office. Her first visit to the sweet-natured therapist had been right after the attack. She'd never forget that awful day. She'd been so terrified, not knowing what to expect and too scared to ask. Immediately, Jackie had put her mind at ease by insisting she call her Dr. Jackie and not Dr. Lewis, joking that Dr. Lewis was her father. She'd gotten her a cup of chamomile tea and they'd talked.

At first, they'd discussed all sorts of things, only slightly touching on the topic of her rape. It wasn't until after a few sessions that Jackie had gotten her to open up. She'd cried while Jackie held her hand and explained there wasn't anything wrong with shedding a few tears. She'd started healing that day, Candice could see that now. And she was grateful to Jackie for getting her through a time in her life when she'd so badly needed someone on her side.

Opening Dr. Jackie's door, Candice walked in and sat in one of the chairs across from the large mahogany desk. It wasn't until Candice jangled her keys as she tossed them into her purse that she managed to capture her doctor's attention.

Jackie, with her long flowing blonde hair and Marilyn Monroe curves, looked up from the patient's file that had her so absorbed. Her mouth dropped open and she whistled.

Candice smiled. She was starting to get used to that expression.

"Someone has something good to tell me," Jackie said in a singsong voice.

Candice's smile turned into a wide grin and she laughed. Actually laughed! How novel was that?

"Oh boy, do I ever."

Jackie got up from her desk and went over to the cozy area she used for her sessions. Candice followed, sitting in one of the matching beige suede chairs opposite Jackie.

"So, spill it, sister. It's got to be pretty darn good for you to come in here wearing that sexy dress."

Candice blushed and her eyes bulged. "Sexy? Seriously?"

Jackie's brows kicked up. "Hell, yes, lady. I nearly didn't recognize you."

Candice wasn't sure she liked that description. Men tended to be more aggressive around sexy women. And she tended to freeze up and panic around aggressive men. Maybe the yellow dress had been a bad idea after all.

Candice smoothed her dress down her thighs, willing it to grow another inch. "I hadn't realized. I mean, I knew the dress was pretty, but—"

Jackie reached out and placed a warm, soft hand on her knee, her voice gentle. "Sexy is a good thing, Candice. And I'd say it's about time you showed off that figure you work so hard to keep."

Jackie was right. Candice just wasn't used to the word "sexy" being associated with her. Learning to accept a compliment without analyzing it to death was one more step in the right direction.

"Thank you, I do feel good in this dress. It's nice to look in the mirror and see me staring back and not some oversized stranger."

"That's my girl. Now, what's brought on all these exciting changes? A man, maybe?"

Jackie grinned again, and she found herself grinning right back. That's what she loved about her therapist. She was so easy to talk to, so candid and open. She didn't pull her punches and she didn't expect anyone else to, either. Candice knew she could tell Jackie anything, and she'd accept and understand. She supposed that was what made Jackie such a good doctor.

"Do you remember that dream I told you about? The one with the gorgeous dark-haired man? The one where he and I...make love?"

"Oh, yeah, I could never forget a dream like that. Positively yummy, girlfriend."

Candice chuckled. "Well, I sort of went out with that man."

Jackie's dumbfounded expression made it clear she thought she'd gone over the bend. "I hadn't realized I'd been dreaming about my boss's brother, Blade Vaughn. He caught me in a bad moment at Lacey's gym Saturday and he sort of tracked me down. Anyway, I ended up telling him all about my rape. He was so wonderful. He took me to his family's house for a cookout, then we came back to my house and we...er, well, it was wonderful. Blade was wonderful. Only now he says he's in love with me, and I got so scared that I—"

Jackie reached a hand out and patted her knee again. "Slow down a bit."

Candice stopped, took a deep breath and explained everything. From the minute she'd lost it in the gym, to her kicking him out Sunday morning. Once Candice was through, she quieted and waited for Dr. Jackie's reaction.

"First, good for you. I'm thrilled that you've finally taken my advice. Going out on a real date with a man is definitely a step in the right direction. You were ready, Candice, it was time."

"Yes," Candice agreed. "I hadn't realized how ready I was until Blade took me to the cookout. I was having such a good time, and it made me a bit melancholy to think of all the fun I'd been missing out on."

"But we don't look back, remember? You did go to the cookout, and you did enjoy what came after, right?"

"Oh yes. Jackie, he was so exciting, so giving." Her voice turned wistful thinking of how incredible Blade had been. "He treated me with such respect. He was so sweetly gentle, and yet so aggressive at the same time. I hadn't known pleasure like that existed between a man and a woman."

"Now that you do, what do you plan to do about it?"

She folded her hands in her lap and said, "This is where things get a bit complicated. He told me he loves me and I'm scared, really scared."

Jackie's face softened as she smiled. "Of course you're scared; any woman would be. But you can't let that fear take you over, Candice. You need to face it; it's the only way you'll get a crack at a real future."

"I know, I know. But where do I go from here? I kicked him out. I told him I needed time to think things through. I just don't want to rush into anything. I want to bring my whole self into this relationship, not half a woman. That wouldn't be fair to Blade."

Jackie laughed. "We all have baggage, sweetie. Even Blade has some. That's just stuff. Stuff's normal. The question now is are you willing to take a chance? To show him you aren't made of glass?"

Candice did want Blade to see her as a strong woman. "Yes."

"Then do something only a confident woman would do. Go to him. Show him how much you want him. Be the one in control of the pleasure this time."

Candice loved the idea, but she was still blank. "I haven't got a single stitch of experience in this area. Absolutely zilch. Got any hints for me?" She'd take any morsel she could get. Candice was already getting excited at the idea of showing Blade a sexier side.

Jackie shrugged. "Give him a private viewing."

She blinked and then blinked again, as if by blinking she'd be able to make sense of what her therapist had just suggested. Thankfully, Jackie took pity on her and spelled it out.

"Give him a striptease." The absolute horror must have shown on her face, because Jackie laughed and said, "You can do this, Candice. There's a wanton little vixen in all of us, trust me."

"Really?" Candice asked, not quite believing she, Candice Warner, could actually strip for a man and have it come off as sexy and enticing. She wasn't shy about the idea, not after everything she and Blade had already shared. Candice simply didn't think she was the sexy stripper type.

"You think I could pull that off?"

Jackie rubbed her hands together. "All you need is the right music, a room with a lock on the door and him in a chair."

As Jackie went on, explaining step-by-step how to strip for her man, Candice sat in fascinated silence, absorbing the gorgeous blonde's obvious knowledge like a sponge. Something in the way Jackie explained exactly what to do, right down to gyrating the hips, moving and swaying to the beat—heck, she even told her which compact disc to buy. Clearly, there was more to Dr. Jackie Lewis than met the eye.

At the end of their session together, which really felt more like friends discussing the best ways to seduce their men, Candice left, promising to call Jackie and let her know how it went. Candice was nervous, but not puke-your-guts-up nervous.

Blade was due for a treat and Candice was going to be the one to feed it to him. First she had a few stops to make. By the end of the workday, Blade was going to get a good long dose of the new and improved Candice Warner.

Chapter Eleven

He was useless. It was already four o'clock and all day he'd been snapping at his men and driving everyone up the wall. And the worst of it was, none of it was their fault. Blade was driving himself crazy and everyone around him because he missed Candice. Since he'd left her house Sunday morning, thoughts of her constantly plagued him.

How she looked naked and writhing beneath him. How she looked when she'd gone down on him in the shower, her face alight with sinful pleasure. He wanted her in a bad way, and nothing was going to fix his ache.

He'd been a good boy and stayed away. Hell, he hadn't even called her, which had nearly killed him. But he wanted to respect her wishes, give her time to adjust to her newfound confidence, be a man of his word by not pushing her into anything she wasn't ready for. She deserved that, his mind knew it, but his gonads weren't so understanding.

Blade wanted Candice so bad he swore he could taste her in his mouth even now, her sweet juices flowing over his tongue like warm honey. He could hear her sighs of rapturous abandon as she came for him. Knowing he was the only man to ever give her that kind of pleasure, to ever hear those sweet moans afterwards, was a powerful feeling.

Once upon a time, the very idea of falling in love would

have sent him stomping off in the opposite direction. He hadn't wanted any woman to crawl under his skin. No woman would ever wield that sort of power over him. Still, when it had happened with Candice, Blade had recognized it for what it was and embraced the feeling like a long lost brother.

Then Candice had sent him home like a ratty mutt who wouldn't go away. Still, he was not giving her up. Blade always got what he wanted. Eventually. And he wanted Candice. Forever. In his bed. In his life. He wanted babies with her, a white picket fence if it made her happy. Who cared, he just wanted her. And he was an impatient man. Blade didn't much care to be left waiting, wallowing in his own misery, while she tried to figure out if she was capable enough to stand on her own two feet. Hell, he could have told her she was more than capable. Any idiot could see that Candice was a strong and intelligent woman. It wouldn't have been easy to go through that trial relating the tale of what had happened all the while having to face not only a jury and a judge, but the bastard who'd raped her as well.

Still, she made him wait. Women! He'd never figure them out.

Just then, Blade heard a huge commotion coming from outside. Whistles? What the hell? They were on a worksite; his men knew better, damn it.

Blade got up from his desk and slammed open the door of the trailer that served as his onsite office. He was more than ready to bust a few heads. It was just the thing he needed to get his mind off Candice.

The sight that greeted him was not a welcome one. All his men were surrounding a petite woman. All he could see of her was a yellow sundress and a wild mane of brown hair. Now why did that hair seem so familiar? Then the yellow apparition turned around and Blade nearly exploded with equal amounts of rage and arousal.

Candice, looking sweet and sassy, surrounded by a motley crew of dirty workers, wasn't panicking? What was that about? He was glad for her, but at the same time, he wanted to rip the faces off all the men staring at her as if she were their last meal.

He strode forward and yanked two men backward, giving Candice room to walk through them and toward him, where she goddamn well belonged.

"Randy, Jake, get the hell out of her way, will ya?"

The smile she graced him with made him feel ten feet tall, as if he could leap over tall buildings and race a few trains.

Jesus H, she was gorgeous. Her dress flirted around her thighs, and sexy amusement lit her eyes. He wanted to whisk her away, keep her all to himself. Other men didn't have the right to breathe the same air as her.

"Blade."

"*Candice.*" He felt needy, and that was never a good emotion for a man.

"Could we go somewhere to talk? Privately?"

Oh, hell, he liked the sound of that—too much. Blade grabbed her hand and hauled her away while his men called out lewd suggestions. He watched Candice, judging her reaction to the men who had cornered her. She was blushing bright red, but she wasn't panicked. Was she finally ready to accept him?

Shit, he hated this.

He couldn't help feeling he was about to experience something truly spectacular only to have it slip away from him again. He didn't want a repeat of yesterday morning, with her sending him away and him wishing he could have just one more minute with her. Just one more minute.

He never begged. Blade wasn't the begging type. So long as he kept telling himself that, he'd be just fine. He could handle this. And she thought she was weak? Hell, she had him mentally on his knees already. Fuck!

Once inside the tiny trailer, Blade slammed the door shut and closed them in. With Candice there, inside his dusty, dingy mobile office, it made him uncomfortable, as if she was too good to be in such an ugly place. He was actually embarrassed to see papers scattered all over his desk, and old, stale coffee sitting in cups, and...shit, was that mold?

Okay, so he wasn't a neat freak.

It wasn't as if he'd invited her here. Come to that, what was she doing here anyway? When he turned to her to ask that very question, the words stuck in his throat. Christ, it was like looking at pure sunshine—it hurt to look straight at it, but you couldn't seem to help yourself. It was so beautiful that you were willing to risk permanent blindness to get a quick peek. Still, she must have had a good reason for coming to an all-male zone like a construction site.

Blade reached out and took hold of Candice's chin, letting his thumb trace her glossy lower lip. The action forced her to stop fussing with her oversized purse and look at him. "Why are you here, Candy girl?"

Candice smiled. There was something different in her expression today, sort of alluring and mysterious. Fascinated and curious to know what she was up to, Blade put more force in his next statement. "You must have had a good reason to brave that dirty male gauntlet outside, so out with it, babe."

Candice's gaze shifted to the door for a split second and then came back to land on him. "Does that door have a lock?"

What was the minx up to? "Yes, but what does that have to do with—" He never got to finish what he was saying. Candice slipped away from him and locked the door to his trailer, then turned around, a slow, come-and-get-it smile on her face.

Oh, he definitely wanted to go and get it, but he wasn't going anywhere near her until she explained why she'd come to him, looking so sweet and flirty.

"I'm working, sweetheart, what do you want?" He didn't mean to sound gruff, as if he didn't want her there, but this new side of her was taking him off guard. He was already hard and throbbing and nothing had even happened yet.

Candice walked away from the door and went straight to his desk. She set her mammoth purse down on top of it with a clunk and rooted around inside. When her hand came out, she was holding a portable compact disc player. She wanted to serenade him?

God, he was majorly confused. And if she moved her ass like that one more time, he'd be on her quicker than a dog on a bone. She went around his desk and grabbed the chair he'd been sitting in, then moved it to the middle of the floor.

"Sit down, Blade."

Okay, he'd play along. It was clear that Candice was on some sort of mission and the quicker she got on with it, the quicker Blade would get some answers.

He crossed the room and sat, arms folded over his chest, feet braced apart as if ready for war.

But Candice only smiled and pushed a button on her player, allowing music to fill the darkly lit room. It wasn't until she came to stand directly in front of him that he started to get the picture.

Locking the door, playing the music—it wasn't a serenade she was interested in. Candice was about to seduce him. A predatory smile slipped over his face and he sat back, prepared to let her. If she wanted to play the lead in an after-dark movie, he'd be glad to be her audience of one.

At first, Candice was stiff and unsure, but it didn't take her long to get into the role of vamp as she began to gently sway to the earthy beat coming from the player. Candice was a natural. With her lithe, toned body, she had an inner fire he knew no other man had ever witnessed. He liked that last part a lot.

Soon he could see her fiddling with her side, and Blade realized she was unzipping the yellow scrap of cotton that pretended to be a dress. In a seductive little shimmy, the dress fell clear to the floor, leaving Candice in a sheer, stretchy...thong? Where the hell did she get a thong? Then again, who the fuck cared where the thong came from. It was where it was now that mattered most.

Three skinny straps wrapped around Candice's smooth hips, connected in the center by a V. A see-thru white V. Blade could see her curls beneath and he could make out the bump of her clit. To make matters even worse, the V was too small, because her curls were peeking out around the edges, making him yearn to lean toward her and give her a good, long lick, right where she needed it most. He could smell her scent already, a potent combination of honeyed arousal and excitement.

The matching bra she wore... Yum. There was no real need for it, except, of course, to entice a man into a horny, begging stupor. And, like a heat-seeking missile, his dick pushed anxiously against the zipper of his fly in a sad attempt to get up close and personal with Candice's scantily clad body.

It wasn't until the song reached a quick, vibrating climax that Candice unhooked the front of the bra and let it slip down her shoulders, elbows and finally to the floor. Now nothing kept him from her creamy perfection, save for that sweet see-thru V.

Blade couldn't sit still and not touch. It was like asking a naughty little boy to keep his hands in his pockets upon entering a candy store. Not gonna happen. And Blade had never been accused of being a good boy.

Reaching out, he grabbed Candice by the hip and scooted her closer. She let him have his way, a sassy smile playing at the corners of her mouth.

"You like teasing me don't you, baby?"

"I'll confess, I've enjoyed watching your eyes heat up and your body go all hard. You're so sexy, Blade."

"I've enjoyed watching you, too. That was the sweetest gift anyone's ever given me." Then he plopped her onto his lap and kissed her.

Blade sank everything he had into that kiss. He wanted her with a wild sort of eagerness that made him almost angry. It wasn't normal to want a woman as badly as he wanted Candice. She sighed, wrapped her arms around his neck and opened her mouth for his demanding tongue. Not taking a chance she might disappear like the ethereal being she was, Blade slipped between her lips and tasted every inch of her dark passion. Candice moaned, and he pushed upward, letting her feel the hard length of his arousal against her bare ass. God, he wanted her. Needed her.

He lifted his head away, enjoying the sound of protest she gave him. 'Bout time she suffered some. He'd been suffering plenty since she'd sent him away.

Blade lifted her to stand in front of him. "Off with the panties, baby." He gave them a yank and Candice twitched her hips, then stepped out of them. Ah, now that was what he'd been missing all day. The sight of Candice Warner, bare-assed and aroused.

He leaned into her and took one protruding nipple into his mouth and sucked, hard. Candice grabbed the back of his head and held him against the fleshy orb. She was every bit as anxious as he was for this. Beyond playing it safe, Blade let one hand slip down her body to cup her mound, swiftly sinking two thick fingers all the way into her tight, wet heat.

"Blade!" Candice shouted. He lifted away from her long enough to see the wide-eyed need on her face. He took her other breast, biting and sucking, while his thumb played over her hard clitoris. Candice moved against his hand, fucking his fingers until suddenly she was crying out his name, her body squeezing and contracting as she came long and hard.

He let her ride out the feelings before he slipped his fingers free of her and stood. His hands went to his belt, watching and gauging Candice's reaction as he freed his cock. When she licked her lips as if imagining his taste, a drop of fluid appeared at the tip. The sight of her standing there so free and uninhibited sent Blade over the edge.

He clutched her hips and swung her around so she faced the desk. "Grab hold of the edge, sweetheart." She never once hesitated, only did as Blade asked, which turned him on further. Blade took hold of Candice's ass and spread her wide, her glistening folds opening, inviting him in. Blade entered her in one smooth stroke, wringing a husky groan from her.

"You fit me perfectly. You're mine, baby," Blade growled, then he leaned over her, bracing his arms on the desk beside her, caging her in, and bit her shoulder.

Candice pushed her hips backward, seeking more of him. "Harder, Blade, please! I need you so bad."

"How bad?" He wanted to hear her beg. It would go a long way in soothing his bruised heart.

"Please, just...just fuck me, Blade!"

He smiled, a rumble of primal male satisfaction rising. "That's what I wanted to hear."

Then he gave it to her, fucking her hard and fast and with a furious need to leave his mark on her. He wanted every man to know she belonged to him. His cock swelled as he thrust into her over and over. He reached around to her front and flicked a thumb around her clit, igniting her passion all over again.

Candice went up in flames, pushing against him. Her hand came to rest over his on her mound as she splintered and shattered. Blade moved faster, thrusting once, twice, until finally he burst wide and filled her.

He took his other hand off the desk and stroked her hair away from her face. Both of them were sweating and shaky. Candice tilted her head sideways, giving him her mouth for a kiss. He took it, softly, lingeringly, before releasing her and pulling out of her. Already the thread between them seemed to snap, and he was at a loss what to do about it.

Blade fixed his clothes then turned Candice around. Redressing her wasn't nearly as much fun as watching her undress for him, but he did get an odd sort of delight in the everyday activity, as if she were letting him into her life just the tiniest bit.

A soft smile lit her face, making him wonder what she was thinking. He wasn't really sure he wanted to know, though. Candice tended to piss him off when she went all contemplative.

As soon as he finished and she was once again covered from his fiery inspection, she turned away and started collecting her things.

So...that was it? She gave him an afternoon show and left?

Anger and hurt welled, making his words harsher than he intended. "What gives, Candy? Why did you come here?"

She turned around so fast, Blade thought she was going to fall over. "Huh?"

Blade shoved a hand through his hair, striving for a calm

he didn't feel. "Yesterday, I told you I love you. You sent me away, needing time. Today, you come in here, give me a little strip show and fuck me senseless, then you just collect your things and leave? What are you playing at? Because I'll tell you, I'm confused as hell."

Candice's face went deathly white, as if someone had sucked all the blood from her, and Blade had the sick feeling she was about to have a panic attack. But before he could say anything, soothe her, tell her he was total dick, she started stammering out her answer.

"I wanted to see if I could...turn you on."

Now that made no sense at all. She *breathed* and he was turned on, damn it. "Come again?" Blade asked. The female sex was a jumble of contradictions.

At the best of times.

She shrugged one shoulder and fidgeted in her dainty white sandals. "You've been doing all the work, and I wanted to show you that I could be seductive."

Blade closed the space between them and wrapped his arms around her. He didn't understand her all the time, but he knew that her coming here, stripping for him, had to be one of the hardest things she'd ever done. "Thank you, sweetheart," he whispered against her ear. "It means a lot that you would come to me like this."

When Candice's eyes met his, he swore he saw love. But he couldn't be certain, because a woman had never loved him before. Well, except his mom and sister, and that didn't really count.

"You liked it? Really?"

He smiled. The woman had no clue how fucking hot she was. He would just have to spend the rest of his life showing her.

"'Like' is too tame. I fucking loved it."

She beamed up at him. Blade wanted to keep her that way, looking at him as if he were the best thing since cotton candy.

"Where do we go from here, Candy girl? What happens now?"

She bit her lip, anxious all at once. "I'm not sure. It's been a long time since I've done anything this aggressive. I need to get my bearings."

He knew that was coming. A day was just not enough time, and yet he'd hoped. He took solace in knowing that she was indeed trying to put her past to rest. Coming to him today proved that much. Dressing in something that fit for a change proved that, too.

"I know, I get it, I really do. Just remember, I love you. That's not subject to change any time in the next fifty years."

She laughed, which was his plan, making him breathe a heavy sigh of relief.

"I know, and thank you for being so wonderful, Blade."

He smiled at her ruefully. "Yeah, I'm real wonderful, taking you against a dirty desk like a crazed animal."

Her eyes heated and turned drowsy. "I liked it. I like you when you go all caveman, Blade. It's very sexy."

He pushed her out of his arms and swatted her on the ass, causing her to jump and squeal. "Knock it off, you little tease." And before she could protest, he picked up her ridiculously oversized purse, and stated, "I'll walk you to your car."

Once she was safely seat-belted in, he kissed her and made her promise to call him. Letting her drive off proved to be the hardest thing Blade had ever done.

He only hoped it was the right thing.

Chapter Twelve

There was no way he could've predicted that coming to Lacey's gym would have run him smack into Candice. Christ, he'd left her not an hour ago, and there she stood, all sexy and hot and flirting like a pro. Blade wanted to shout to the world he was so proud of her transformation.

She wore a pair of those tight black shorts that pretty much showed her ass to any and all, and another of her workout tops. This one was hot pink. He wanted to strip her naked, fuck her hard, then kiss her for hours. It didn't seem to matter that he'd just come inside her. How could she work out after such a vigorous afternoon? Against his desk, no less!

Even from across the room, Candice radiated confidence. But she was so busy chatting, she didn't realize the shmuck wasn't listening to a word she said. He was more concerned about her pretty tits. While Blade really wanted to gouge out the guy's eyes, he couldn't help but marvel at how much she'd changed.

"Hey, Blade! Hello? Are you even listening to me?"

Belatedly, he realized Lacey had been talking to him the entire time he'd been watching Candice. "Uh, what?"

"I asked why the big grin. You haven't stopped smiling since you spied Candice."

"She's not panicking."

"I know and it's wonderful. She's like a different person."

Lacey's voice was full of wonder, compelling him to correct her statement. "Not different, just more secure. More comfortable in her own skin."

"You've been very good for her."

He looked at his sister and winked. "Damn straight."

Lacey rolled her eyes. "You're impossible."

Blade laughed, but when he looked back at Candice and saw the guy touch her on the arm, he tensed. "Time to step up to the plate."

"No fighting in my gym!"

"Wouldn't dream of it," he growled. She might want to move on with her life, test out her newfound confidence, but he was determined to be right there beside her.

Within a few long strides, Blade was across the gym floor and wrapping a proprietary arm around Candice's waist. She let out a startled squeak.

"Blade!"

"Hi, baby," he whispered, "I missed you."

He leaned down and placed a possessive kiss to her luscious lips for all to see. When he let Candy up for air, he noticed the pretty-boy in the muscle shirt had moved on. Smart guy. Blade dismissed him and concentrated on the more pressing problem. Candice and her role in his future.

He touched the tip of her nose and asked, "Have you been enjoying yourself?"

"What on earth are you doing here?"

He bent low and said, "I came to see Lacey, but I was more entertained by your flirting."

Her eyes narrowed. "You were watching the entire time?"

He grabbed her hand and walked her to an unused aerobics room, then let her go long enough to pull her into his arms. His cock nestled between her legs, and his arousal flared to life.

"Blade, answer my question."

He tamped down his urges and said, "Yes, I watched. You looked like you'd been doing it all your life."

"Are you angry?"

"I'm not exactly thrilled about the guy ogling your chest, but I'm not angry at you for testing out your courage."

"You don't understand."

"Then make me understand, sweetheart."

"Can you let me go first?"

He grinned. "Nope. I like you in my arms." He looked around for a place where they could be alone, then proceeded to drag her off to a back room. One with a door.

He knew the gym's layout, and the room he took her to was an extra private workout room. It was seldom used. Blade kicked the door shut and locked them in, then lowered her to her feet. Blade pushed her up against the door. "Now, explain. And make it quick, because I want you again. I've wanted to fuck you the instant you sashayed out of my dirty office," he said crudely.

"I love you."

Well, hell, if that didn't just throw a guy for a loop. It was exactly what he'd hoped to hear coming from her sweet lips, but didn't think he would. Still, she'd never had the chance to play the field. He needed to be sure she wasn't leaping too fast. "What about the pretty boy?"

"He doesn't hold a candle to you."

Her soft voice nearly did him in. Seemed that was all it took for his brain to head south and imagine her naked and spread out for his pleasure.

"You love me?" Blade asked, needing to hear it again, then realized she was practically bubbling with excitement. "So, that guy didn't mean anything to you?" He was thankful it hadn't been more. He would have died if it'd been more.

"We were just talking. That's all, I swear. I felt confident at the construction site today. Those men surrounded me, but I knew you were there and you'd keep me safe. So, it wasn't really a true test. I needed to know I could do it on my own. I needed that, Blade."

With her arms and hands now free, she started caressing his chest, his abs, and Blade became pleasantly distracted.

"I just needed to be sure. To know I wasn't bringing all my baggage into this relationship." Candice reached down and cupped him through his jeans. He nearly stopped breathing. "I want us to start fresh, and I really, really want the past to stay buried."

She squeezed, and Blade groaned.

"I think I've actually accomplished that, because I do love you," she said on a hoarse sigh as she went to her knees and began to unbuckle his belt.

He found his voice. "Whoa, baby." She looked up at him with such innocence and curiosity that Blade's heart did a flip. "I want to hear you say that again."

He reached down and pulled her back to her feet, then yanked and tugged until her workout top was over her head and her beautiful breasts were bare. "Tell me you love me, sweetheart. Let me hear you say it."

"I love you, Blade."

Her breathless eagerness was music to his ears and a balm

to his heart. He tugged at her shorts and panties, grappling and twisting them over her shoes, then tossed them aside. "Ever have sex in a public place before?"

"Of course not."

She sounded scandalized, but excited. "Good," he grunted, feeling strangely territorial. "Spread your legs for me." She quickly obeyed. "No more testing, Candy girl. You passed with flying colors. No need to beat a dead horse. Understand?"

"Yes, Blade. Just...please, I need you!"

He lowered himself to the floor, then reached around her to smooth both palms over the firm globes of her ass. Without warning, Blade wiggled his index finger between and stroked her pucker.

"Blade!"

"Shh, be quiet unless you want everyone to hear you," he ground out as he slid his finger up and down her slick folds. "Do you like that, baby?"

"God, yes," she responded softly, then added, "but if you don't get on with it, I'm going to show you a few of the moves your sister has taught me."

"Sounds intriguing," Blade murmured as he parted her and licked obediently. His tongue probed in and out, fucking her, eating at her, driving her wild and making him crazy with desire. He lifted one hand and covered her mouth as she began to buck against his face, moaning uncontrollably. Suddenly, Candice let herself go as she came long and hard, her scream of completion muffled against his palm.

She was the most beautiful creature he'd ever set eyes on.

He stood and quickly undid his belt and jeans. Taking himself in hand, Blade knelt slightly, accommodating for his height, then slid into her wet heat. "Christ, I love you, Candice

Warner, so damn much."

"Oh, yes, Blade, I love you, too!"

Blade grasped her around the waist and lifted her. "Wrap those sexy legs around me, sweetheart."

Candice did as instructed, then rode him hard and fast. He leaned down and suckled her nipple, nipping and tugging, frantic to take all of her at once. She started to tighten and quiver around his cock, milking him with her inner muscles. It drove Blade over the edge.

He smothered his own moans against her throat. As his body spun out of control, he realized she was right there with him, holding him tight and flying over that precipice safely tucked in his arms.

They stayed like that for a moment longer, breathing heavily, loving each other until there was a tentative knock on the door.

"What!" Blade yelled.

"Either you two are attempting to beat the door down, or something very naughty is going on," Lacey said in a wicked voice.

"Get lost," Blake growled. He kissed Candice on her shoulder, her collarbone and finally her neck. She whimpered.

"Blade?" Lacey again, interrupting them for the second time.

"Go away, Lacey!" he barked.

"Everyone out here can hear you two. The doors aren't soundproof, you big lug!" She giggled as only a little sister can, then moved on.

"Shit," he muttered, then another thought occurred. One more pressing than hollow doors.

"Candy?"

"Hmm?" she answered sleepily.

"You know, you could be pregnant. The pill isn't always enough, baby," he said gently. Candice looked away, and he tugged her chin back to him, forcing her to face reality. "Candy?"

"I-I wouldn't mind, Blade." She said it so quietly, Blade had to strain to hear. His heart nearly soared to the heavens.

"I was really hoping you'd say that." He kissed her firmly, thrusting his tongue between her lips, making her tremble and sigh.

To Blade's way of thinking, life didn't get any better than being loved by the woman of your dreams.

About the Author

To learn more about Anne Rainey, please visit http://annerainey.com. Send an email to Anne at anne@annerainey.com or join her Yahoo! group to join in the fun with other readers as well as Anne! http://groups.yahoo.com/group/rb_afterdark

GREAT cheap fun

Discover eBooks!

THE FASTEST WAY TO GET THE HOTTEST NAMES

Get your favorite authors on your favorite reader, long before they're out in print! Ebooks from Samhain go wherever you go, and work with whatever you carry—Palm, PDF, Mobi, and more.

Samhain publishing Ltd

CPSIA information can be obtained at www.ICGtesting.com
Printed in the USA
BVOW030505041212

307234BV00001B/52/P